PUFFIN BOOKS

STARLIGHT
Stables

BUSH BOLTS

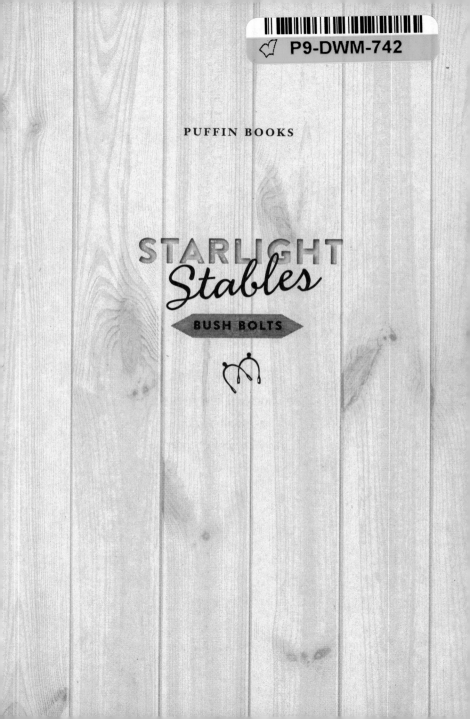

SORAYA NICHOLAS

STARLIGHT
Stables

BUSH BOLTS

PUFFIN BOOKS

PUFFIN BOOKS

UK | USA | Canada | Ireland | Australia
India | New Zealand | South Africa | China

Penguin Books is part of the Penguin Random House group of companies
whose addresses can be found at global.penguinrandomhouse.com.

Penguin
Random House
Australia

First published by Penguin Random House Australia Pty Ltd, 2016

10 9 8 7 6 5 4 3 2 1

Design by Marina Messiha © Penguin Random House Australia Pty Ltd
Cover photograph © Caitlin Maloney, Ragamuffin Pet Photography
Author photograph p172 by Carys Monteath
Printed and bound in Australia by Griffin Press, an accredited ISO AS/NZS 14001
Environmental Management Systems printer.

National Library of Australia Cataloguing-in-Publication data:

Nicholas, Soraya, author.
Starlight stables: bush bolts/Soraya Nicholas.

ISBN 978 0 1433 0862 1 (paperback)

For children.
Ponies – Juvenile fiction.
Horse shows – Juvenile fiction.
Friendship – Juvenile fiction.

A823.4

penguin.com.au

For Mackenzie & Hunter,
my budding little horse riders!
I also need to make special mention
of the real Missy, who features in this book.
She's the best pony our family
could have wished for.

CHAPTER ONE

Three Becomes Four

'I can't believe you're actually coming with me!' Poppy laughed as she jumped onto the bed beside her best friend Sarah and flopped down on her stomach.

'*You* can't believe it? Imagine how I feel!' Sarah swatted at Poppy, but Poppy rolled out of the way, smiling.

'You're going to love it,' said Poppy, thinking about all the things she couldn't wait to show her. She'd been trying to convince Sarah to visit Starlight Stables forever, even though she knew her best friend wasn't exactly horse crazy. Poppy was pretty sure Sarah had only finally said yes because she was so curious about Milly and Katie.

'I know.' Sarah was grinning back now as she tucked her long, glossy black hair behind her ear, eyes full of excitement. 'It's going to be awesome meeting your new riding friends.'

'Don't forget Crystal!' Poppy joked, knowing that Sarah would want to put off meeting any horse, even Poppy's beautiful pony, for as long as possible.

'And your aunt Sophie seems pretty cool,' Sarah continued. Poppy knew she had ignored her on purpose.

'She is cool.' Poppy had forgotten that Sarah met Aunt Sophie when she came to stay. She tried not to think about that time, after her dad had died and her mum went all quiet. Everything was much better since Aunt Sophie had come and helped her mum. Poppy enjoyed being at home now, even if she did spend most of the time looking forward to being back at Starlight Stables.

She poked Sarah. 'It's going to be a bit of a squash in my room there, with Milly and Katie bunking on camp beds too, but it'll be fine.'

'I don't care about being squished.' Sarah sighed. 'It's just the horses. I wish I loved them like you do.'

'Me too,' Poppy said, rolling off the bed and

opening her suitcase. She was hoping that once Sarah actually spent some time with the horses, she'd change her mind. Sarah loved smaller animals, but for some reason she just wasn't interested in riding. Poppy had decided she was going to change all that.

'Come on, help me finish packing,' she said. Her friend was still lying on her tummy, ankles crossed in the air behind her, munching happily on some biscuits. Poppy held out her hand for one. She had no idea what they were called, but she loved the little chewy chocolate snacks that Sarah's grandma often sent over from China.

'Okay, so I've got a spare pair of jods for you and my old riding boots.' Poppy threw them into the suitcase alongside her two pairs of good jods, boots and a few T-shirts. Finally, she tossed in her hoodie. 'I think that's all. Aunt Sophie has all the other stuff you'll need like a helmet, and . . .' She bit down on a biscuit, savouring it as she mentally ran through everything her friend might need. 'Yep, we're good to go.'

'I hope they like me,' Sarah said, holding out the packet again. Poppy took a few more.

'Milly and Katie already think you're awesome after you came up with the idea to catch Jessica out,' Poppy said. 'Your idea saved the day!'

'Has Jessica left Starlight Stables now? Like for good? I still can't believe what she did to your horse.'

'Can we not talk about Jessica?' A shudder ran through Poppy just thinking about how close she'd been to losing her gorgeous Crystal.

Sarah jumped off the bed and threw the empty biscuit packet in the trash. 'Okay. But back to the horses . . .'

'Just give it a go.' Poppy zipped up her case and then slung an arm around Sarah's shoulders. 'It's going to be awesome.'

'Yeah, says the horse nut!' Sarah rolled her eyes.

Poppy laughed. 'You'll be great. If you don't like it, we'll just do something else.' Of course, there was no way *she* wasn't riding Crystal this weekend, but if Sarah still hated horses once she'd given riding a go, then Poppy wasn't about to make her miserable by forcing her on a trail ride.

Poppy thought back to all the times Sarah had sat with her, watching DVDs and feeding her dumplings, when Poppy was worried about her mum and didn't want to leave her home alone. She was sure Sarah would have much rather been out doing other stuff. This was only one weekend, and Sarah had been her best friend forever. Poppy was desperate to show her how much fun her aunt and uncle's place was. And she had a grand plan to get Sarah visiting Starlight more often, maybe even over the Christmas holidays. She hated not seeing her for weeks at a time while she was there.

'Girls! Time to go. We've got ten minutes to get to the station and buy your tickets before the train leaves!'

Poppy squeezed Sarah in excitement and grabbed her suitcase. She couldn't wait to get back to Starlight Stables.

Poppy bit down on her bottom lip as the car turned slowly into the driveway. The tyres crunched over the gravel, and Poppy looked at the open gates with Starlight Stables emblazoned on them, the big trees waving at them in the breeze all the way in. She glanced at Sarah, who was looking out the window as they passed the wooden fences, then the show-jumping arena with the perfect red-and-white striped poles.

When the car pulled up outside the stables, Poppy couldn't keep her mouth shut any longer.

'What do you think?' she asked excitedly. There was no way Sarah wasn't impressed.

'It's really pretty,' Sarah said, smiling back at her.

'Out you get, girls,' Aunt Sophie said, turning in the front seat and winking at Poppy.

Poppy flung the door open and grabbed Sarah's hand, tugging her out with her.

'I'll grab your bags,' Aunt Sophie called out. 'Go and see that pony of yours.'

Poppy was dying to see Crystal, and she grinned at Sarah again, still holding her hand. 'Ready to take a look around?'

Sarah shrugged. 'Sure.'

Poppy was convinced they were going to have an amazing weekend as she dragged Sarah after her.

'These are the stables,' she said as they passed them. 'We turn the horses out when we're here and only stable them when they're in work. I mean, when we're bringing them in to ride.'

'Uh-huh,' Sarah said.

Poppy hurried them past the big wooden stable block and barn and down to the first paddock. Her heart started beating fast like it always did when she was about to see Crystal, and she quickly called out, spotting her in the distance grazing with the others.

'Crystal!'

Crystal pricked her ears and lifted her head. Then she started to trot towards them. The other ponies followed.

'Should we run?' Sarah asked, sounding worried and moving to stand behind Poppy.

'No, they'll slow down soon.' Poppy had forgotten that Sarah might be scared. 'I promise.'

Crystal slowed to a walk and approached hesitantly, until Poppy held out her hand and she sniffed it. Then she relaxed and Poppy moved to stand beside her.

'Isn't she gorgeous?' Poppy slung her arm around Crystal's neck, trying not to laugh at the expression on her friend's face.

'Um, I guess. For a horse.' Sarah wrinkled her nose and kept her distance from Crystal, watching her like she was a wild beast.

'She just wants a pat,' Poppy said, unable to understand Sarah's reaction. She loved *everything* about horses, even if it was just hanging out with them in the stables. 'She's so sweet that I can put a biscuit between my teeth and she'll eat it straight from my mouth. Wanna see?'

Sarah shook her head. 'No way, that's gross.'

Poppy rolled her eyes and gave Crystal a big hug, passing her pony the biscuit she had in her pocket. 'It's not gross – horses don't have bad germs or anything.'

'Argh!'

Sarah's wail made Poppy jump. She spun around to see Milly's horse nudging Sarah roughly with his nose. Sarah leapt forward and grabbed Poppy, and Poppy couldn't help it – she burst out laughing.

'That's just Joe,' she snorted, when the little chestnut pony tried to nudge Sarah again. Poppy dug another biscuit from her pocket and held it out to him. 'He's Milly's pony, and he's not used to anyone not liking him.'

'He nudged me hard! I felt his teeth!' Sarah exclaimed as she linked her arm tightly through Poppy's.

'He's not going to eat you. He just thinks you have treats for him.'

Poppy couldn't help but giggle again when Sarah glared at her.

'I'm not scared of him,' she insisted. 'I just . . . wasn't expecting him to be so badly behaved. And so smelly.'

'They smell delicious,' Poppy disagreed, snuggling up to Crystal and giggling when Joe stretched his neck out and tried to snuffle Sarah again. 'If I could bottle the smell of horse, I'd wear it as a perfume every day.'

'You are *so* gross, and if you did that I'd never sit beside you at school,' Sarah laughed. 'Come on, let's go explore some more of the farm. And I really want to meet Casper.'

Poppy sighed and let go of Crystal, pushing Joe out of the way for a third time.

'Okay. Sorry, girl,' Poppy said to Crystal. 'But Sarah's my guest, so I have to let her be annoying and drag me away.'

She flashed a grin at her best friend, but Sarah was already walking quickly back across the paddock.

Poppy caught up with Sarah as she fumbled with the gate. Poppy leaned over to help her, unlatching it and letting them both through.

Poppy smiled and looped an arm over Sarah's shoulders, casting just a quick glance back at her pony. 'Come on, I'm going to make sure you have a great weekend, and you'll be happy you came once you meet the others.'

The others were Poppy's *other* best friends. When her aunt and uncle had given her Crystal, her first pony, they'd also given scholarships to Milly and Katie, meaning they got their own ponies to ride, too.

The three of them had fast become the best of friends, and Poppy couldn't wait to see them again. Since the Christmas holidays they'd seen each other every second weekend, but this time they had Monday off school for Labour Day, which meant three whole days of riding.

'My mum told me this weekend would be *character building* when I told her I wasn't sure about coming,' Sarah said. 'She's so weird sometimes. But I think she was happy that I wanted to give riding a go.'

'That's what my dad used to say about anything I didn't want to do!' Poppy giggled, relieved she could finally talk about her dad without bursting into tears. He'd died less than a year ago, and she still missed him so much, but it was getting easier to think about him without feeling too upset.

They walked, arm in arm, past another paddock where Aunt Sophie's big horse Jupiter was turned out. Usually Poppy would have stopped to give him a pat, but she doubted Sarah wanted to meet *another* horse.

'Is that one of them?'

Poppy looked up, waving the second she saw Milly getting out of her mum's car.

'Milly!' she called. 'Come and meet Sarah!'

Milly's grin was huge and her braces glinted in the sun as she hauled her bag from the boot and dropped it on the gravel driveway. Her dark curly hair was loose and wild, and she was already dressed in her jods and riding boots.

'Look who I brought with me!' Milly cried.

Poppy laughed when she saw Katie appear from behind the back of the car. She hadn't been expecting them to arrive together.

'Katie!' she cried excitedly.

Katie was the complete opposite of Milly. Her long blonde hair was tied back in a pretty fishplait that hung gracefully over her shoulder. Poppy thought her friend was starting to look a lot like Aunt Sophie now that she braided it the exact same way. She was in her jodhpurs, too, helmet under her arm and a bag in the other hand.

'Hey!' Katie called, smiling.

Sarah tried to let go of Poppy's hand, but Poppy wasn't going to allow her to hang back. She dragged her along, clasping her hand tight again, wanting her to meet the girls properly. She'd been so excited for days and she wasn't used to Sarah being so shy. She definitely didn't want to think about how awful it would be if they didn't all like each other!

'Come on, they'll love you,' Poppy whispered.

Sarah's smile was small, but Poppy saw it. She knew why Sarah was being quiet. She was worried Poppy's horsey friends wouldn't like her, but Sarah didn't realise how excited Milly and Katie were to finally meet her. How could they not like her when she was Poppy's best friend? She was fun and silly and kind; aside from not being horsey, there was nothing about her not to like. It was weird to see Sarah unsure of herself, when at home she was the one who always took charge.

'You been to see the horses yet?' Milly asked, jumping the last step and throwing her arms around Poppy for a big hug.

Poppy dropped Sarah's hand and hugged Milly back, giggling when Katie joined in the group hug, their arms tangling around each other.

Conscious of not wanting Sarah to feel left out, Poppy stepped back and held out one arm.

'Ta da!' she said with a laugh. 'This is the famous Sarah.'

Milly instantly leapt toward Sarah and pulled her in for a big hug.

'We love you!' she declared dramatically. 'You saved us from the evil Jessica!'

Poppy smiled, grateful to Milly for being, well, Milly. She felt herself relax. Any worries she had over her friends getting along instantly evaporated. Katie pushed Milly out of the way and awkwardly opened her arms to hug Sarah too.

'Ignore Milly,' she said. 'I'm Katie. As in the *not crazy* one.'

'Sarah,' Sarah mumbled once Katie had let go of her. 'Nice to meet you.'

'Who are you calling "crazy"?' Milly demanded, hands on hips.

Poppy elbowed Milly. 'You!'

Milly rolled her eyes and Poppy was happy to see Sarah stifle a giggle.

'Fine. I'm off to see Joe. Who's coming with me?'

'Is he the one who shoved me?' Sarah asked.

Poppy winced and was about to answer when Milly planted her hands on her hips. 'Joe would never shove anyone,' she declared.

'He did,' said Sarah. 'We were –'

'He was just excited to see us,' Poppy interrupted quickly. Just when she'd thought the first meeting was going so well between her friends, and now Milly was looking upset.

'I'm dying to see Cody. Sarah, do you want to come with us?' Katie's smile was kind and sweet as always as she put an arm around Sarah. Poppy knew she was trying to smooth things over.

Sarah looked at Poppy. 'Um, Poppy was about to show me around. I'm not that into horses so I was going to meet the dog.'

Milly made a face like she was about to say something, but Poppy quickly jumped in.

'Maybe later . . .' She shrugged apologetically. The one thing she wanted more than anything else in the world was to go back down and smother Crystal with kisses and cuddles and head out for a ride straightaway. But she couldn't just leave Sarah now that the others had arrived, not when she was trying to make it fun for her. 'We'll catch up with you two soon. I've already been down to see Crystal, and I want to finish showing Sarah around the farm.'

Milly frowned and gave her a puzzled look. 'You sure?'

Poppy nodded firmly. 'Yup.'

'Hi, girls!' Aunt Sophie appeared from the stables. She was wearing her trademark pink shirt with the sleeves rolled up, and cream jodhpurs. 'Mark has a surprise for you all if you want to pop into the garage. He's dying to show you something.'

Poppy felt her eyebrows shoot up and she swapped excited glances with the others.

'What is it, Mrs D?' Milly asked, her brown eyes huge.

Aunt Sophie winked and walked away. 'Go and see your ponies and then come down to find out,' she called over her shoulder.

Milly and Katie raced off to the paddocks, arms pumping as they tried to outrun each other. Poppy was torn, wanting desperately to follow them, but also wanting Sarah to love it here.

Milly glanced back, so Poppy linked her arm through Sarah's and walked her in the opposite direction. It was only one weekend, after all, and she needed to do whatever it took to make Sarah love Starlight Stables, even if that meant spending less time with her pony. She could give Crystal extra cuddles later to make up for it, but right now they could be first to find out what Uncle Mark's surprise was.

'Want to go see what it is?' she asked.

That put a huge smile on Sarah's face and Poppy was relieved to see her looking happy – even if it was because she didn't have to go and hang out with the horses again.

She'd imagined that Sarah would arrive at

Starlight, see how gorgeous Crystal and the other ponies were, and change her mind about horses. But she was beginning to realise maybe that wasn't going to happen. Or at least, not without a plan.

'What do you think it is?' Sarah asked, obviously curious.

'I'll bet it's something to do with animals,' Poppy said. 'You know, because he's a vet.'

Sarah leaned into her as they walked off. 'I wish I liked horses as much as you do. I'm not just trying to be a pain in the butt.' She sighed. 'I can't wait to meet your uncle though and find out about his job. It must be so cool being a vet.'

Poppy hugged her tight. 'You've been an awesome friend. When Dad died and Mum was bad, you were the only person on the planet who knew what was really going on, except for Aunt Sophie. I don't care if you don't like horses.'

She was telling the truth – Sarah had been the best friend ever. At home they had a blast hanging out at the park and going to St Kilda beach, so it didn't matter. Not to mention all the awesome Chinese food Sarah's mum always made for them. She'd just thought that Sarah would feel differently once she actually did some horsey stuff.

'So does that mean I can explore the farm on foot when you guys ride?' Sarah asked, her voice hopeful. 'Take the dog for a big walk?'

'No way!' Poppy answered, shaking her head. 'You're riding whether you like it or not. There's no way Milly would forgive me if I didn't force you onto a horse.'

Sarah groaned. 'I thought we'd get here and you'd do stuff with horses and I'd do something else.'

'Never. I was hoping *you'd* get here and be desperate to ride!' Poppy replied, skipping ahead then turning around so she could walk backwards and look at Sarah. 'Besides, if you don't ride, you won't get to go on crazy Milly adventures with us. She always comes up with something fun to do.'

'Oh yeah, I remember hearing all about those "adventures". I don't remember you calling them all fun!' Sarah mocked.

Poppy giggled. 'Come on, let's go hug a baby possum or something else cute. That'll make you feel way better.'

She grabbed Sarah's hand again, getting used

to having to tow her around the farm. Sarah might not love horses, but Poppy was determined to find something about Starlight Stables that her best friend liked. Poppy had some thinking to do – she wanted to help Sarah fall in love with the farm. She just had to figure out how . . .

Uncle Mark's Surprise

'Hi, girls,' Uncle Mark said in a low voice when they walked into the garage to find him.

Poppy couldn't believe the transformation. Last time she'd been in there it had been full of tools and Mark's vet equipment, but now those things were stacked away in one corner and there was a big fan in the middle of the room, a large high stainless steel table against one wall, and some sort of divider that was hiding one corner.

Mark was crouched down with his back to them. Poppy held out her hand to stop Sarah from moving, knowing that he must be doing something important.

Mark rose slowly and when he turned around Poppy couldn't stop her grin, especially when Sarah grabbed her hand.

'Ohmygosh that's so cute!' Poppy whispered, stopping herself from rushing forward and forcing herself to move as slowly as she could towards Uncle Mark.

'This is awesome!' Sarah whispered.

'Not bad handy work, huh?' Mark murmured, his smile impossible to ignore.

Poppy stopped a few feet from him, her eyes glued to the hilarious little joey pouches he was wearing. It took her a while to realise they'd been sewn on to the front of his flannel shirt. They were made from cotton, and she could see tiny furry legs sticking out of one pouch, and a little nose poking out of the other. Her uncle was such a dag when it came to animals.

'Did you make that?' Sarah asked. 'That's so cool!'

Poppy took another step closer to inspect the baby staring at her. She wasn't sure straightaway what it was, but it looked cute with its little black nose and huge brown eyes.

'He's adorable,' Sarah whispered, and Poppy grinned when she realised how excited Sarah was.

'Sophie came up with them after I showed her a photo the wildlife centre gave me,' Uncle Mark said. 'I need to keep their body warmth up and they like being in the pouch – it's how their mothers would have carried them.'

'Are their mothers dead?' Sarah asked.

Poppy cringed, knowing what he was going to say before he even said it. There was only one reason Uncle Mark would ever separate a tiny baby from its mum.

'Yeah,' he said, glancing at Poppy with that 'You okay?' look. She smiled back to reassure him. Everyone was still so weird around her when they talked about death, but she got why. She was getting better at reassuring people with just a smile, but knowing these little animals had lost a parent did make her sad, and it wasn't just because her own dad had died. It would have made her super sad anyway, even if her dad was still here.

'Where did you find them?' Sarah asked.

'They're brushtail possums,' Mark said. 'Both their mothers died in a bushfire a couple of hours' drive away, but the local animal hospital and volunteer carer centres were all full, so I offered to take on the overflow. It's been our worst bushfire season in years, and I might have to take in more animals yet.'

'Do you put them in there to feed them?' Poppy asked, glancing sideways and seeing the little bottles of milk and syringes on the table.

'It's the easiest way because they're comfortable and they stay still, plus it keeps them warm,' he told the girls. 'Then when I'm done, I just wriggle out of this and hang it over there, so they can stay tucked up.'

Poppy couldn't take her eyes off the little creatures. She'd never seen a baby possum up close before.

'Can we feed them?' Sarah asked, standing close to Poppy, their shoulders jammed tight as they looked at the babies.

'How about you girls watch me do these little guys? I need to syringe it directly into their mouths, but you can take turns bottle feeding the kangaroo joeys.'

There were baby kangaroos too? Poppy glanced

at Sarah and they both nodded eagerly.

'I've got them all hanging in pouches behind there,' Mark said, indicating with his head for them to look behind him. Poppy realised suddenly what the wall divider was for – a quieter, darker area for the babies to sleep. 'They're easy to feed, so long as you hold the bottle tight.'

'What's going on . . . ?' Milly burst through the door, her voice booming loud as usual.

'Shhh,' Sarah hissed at the same time as Uncle Mark turned around with a warning finger to his lips.

Milly clamped her hand over her mouth, but her eyes were wide as she stared at the pouches.

'What is this place?' Katie asked, whispering.

Mark grinned. 'Welcome back, Katie,' he said. Then he turned to Milly. 'Hi there, Noisy.' Milly put her hands on her hips, but Mark just laughed quietly and shook his head. 'Keep your voices nice and low in here, girls. We have a lot of young joeys that are easily frightened. And we have a wombat sleeping off an anaesthetic too. I had to do minor surgery on one of his legs.'

Katie and Milly shuffled closer to Mark so they

were standing beside Poppy. 'Did you rescue these babies from those bushfires?' Katie asked.

Mark was busy doing something to the syringes of milk so Poppy quickly answered for him. 'He took them in when the other places were full. He's said we can feed the kangaroo joeys.'

'Kangaroos!' Milly said excitedly.

'Shhh,' Poppy and Katie both hissed at the same time.

Milly wrapped her arms around herself and let out a dramatic, deep breath. 'I'm not used to being so quiet.'

'Yeah, we know!' Katie whispered back.

They watched as Mark gently fed the possum joeys. Poppy loved seeing him work with animals; he was so kind to them and she'd loved listening to all his stories about looking after every animal – from horses and cattle to cats and wildlife – when she'd been on rounds with him in the past. If she couldn't be a professional horse rider when she grew up, then she definitely wanted to be a vet so she could help animals. She bet Sarah was super impressed, too.

Poppy crossed the room to the stainless steel

table and collected one of the bottles Mark had already made up. 'Is this what we feed them?' she asked in a low voice, eager to get closer to the cute animals.

He nodded but didn't take his eyes off the joeys he was feeding. 'Give me a sec and I'll show you what to do. Then maybe you girls can do some of the feeds for me while you're here.'

Poppy almost burst with excitement. She loved helping out with all the animals, and the idea she might get to feed *wild* baby ones? She couldn't stop grinning.

'Sarah, do you want to go first?' Mark asked. 'The clinics that are set up with all the equipment required for major burns and surgeries have all the adult animals, so we have just a few babies that we can easily tend to.'

Poppy was desperate to be the first to hold the bottle. But her friend was way out of her comfort zone coming to spend a weekend with horses, so it was kind of the least she could do, letting her go first.

'You bet!' Sarah grinned, stepping forward. She was the only one not wearing jods. Instead, she was dressed in jeans and a T-shirt, her jeans scrunched up at the knee where she'd tucked them inside Poppy's old scuffed riding boots.

Sarah started peppering Mark with questions about the animals and how to look after them. Her face glowed and Poppy couldn't help noticing she seemed much happier here than in the horse paddock. Poppy smiled. So long as Sarah was happy on the farm, Poppy was happy, even if it wasn't riding related.

While they were chatting and feeding the possums, Poppy saw Milly sidling quietly away. Poppy followed, curious to take a look.

In the corner that was sectioned off, some wood pieces had been bolted to the garage wall. Two large pouches hung from the wood and a makeshift fence surrounded the area. Poppy could just see gangly legs peeking out of the pouches. It looked like a tight fit!

'They must be the kangaroos in there,' Poppy whispered, pointing.

'I know. Cool, huh?'

A hand closed over Poppy's shoulder and she turned to see Sarah.

'You should have mentioned the baby animals,' her friend whispered. 'Then I would have come to Starlight Stables sooner!'

Poppy grinned. Maybe she'd have to look out for animals to rescue all the time if it meant Sarah would keep coming back.

'Just let me toilet these little guys, then I'll be with you,' Mark said from the other side of the room.

'Toilet them?' Poppy asked.

'Yuk,' Milly muttered as they all watched Mark massage first one baby possum, then another.

'Their mother would have licked them, to get them to go after feeding. So I massage them like this . . .' Uncle Mark explained. 'It's just poop, Milly. Nothing to be disgusted about. Seeing them grow and thrive makes it all worth it.'

Milly didn't look convinced, but Sarah nodded, totally engrossed in what Mark was saying. Poppy couldn't have cared less about the poop part, and she was impressed that Sarah didn't seem to care either. Poppy picked up horse poo all the time, and she'd seen her uncle do way more disgusting things for work, like put his arm inside a cow to yank its baby calf out when it got stuck during birth.

Once he was finished, Mark hung the possums up on the makeshift stand and collected the two remaining bottles. These ones were more like human baby bottles rather than the big plastic syringes with tiny teats on the end he'd been using to feed the possums.

'Do you know what happened to their mothers?' Katie asked.

Mark gestured for them to follow and opened the temporary fence he had in place around where the kangaroos were. 'One of these babies was found on its own, badly burned across his paws and seriously dehydrated. He's lucky to be alive. The other, he was inside his mum's pouch. She was dead, but this little guy miraculously survived.'

Poppy watched Mark, took note of how slowly he approached the pouches and the way he held the bottles. She loved the idea of helping him. 'Poppy, you want to go first?' he asked.

Poppy couldn't believe her luck. She took one of the bottles, holding it the same way Mark did.

'I've got them hanging on this wall because there's a heat pad fitted beneath the blanket. The pouches get the right amount of warmth from it.'

The joeys stuck their heads out, the pouches giving them just enough wriggle room as they peered from their spots. The one Poppy was about to feed hungrily latched on to the teat, and she had to hold it firmly to stop it from being pulled out of her hand! She couldn't take her eyes off his skinny legs, thick fur, and chocolate-brown eyes – he was gorgeous!

'It's pretty special, Pops,' her uncle said, winking at her as she copied everything he was doing.

'It's amazing.' She smiled down at the beautiful joey as he suckled. 'Is it special milk?'

'Yes,' Mark replied. 'Special milk for marsupial orphans. We'd do them more harm than good feeding them cow's milk.'

'Can I have a turn now?' Sarah asked eagerly.

Poppy nodded and waited for Sarah's hand to close over the bottle before she removed hers. They both stood there and watched, hardly breathing. Poppy wished she could stroke it's beautiful fur but she knew it would frighten him.

'Will you keep them as pets?' Katie asked Mark softly.

'Sadly, no. I'll do my bit until the animal rescue centre can take them, then they'll aim to release them into the wild when they can. But there could be more fires if the drought doesn't break soon.'

Poppy hoped bushfire season would be over soon. The idea of a fire coming close to Starlight Stables terrified her. But if Mark did get more animals, she'd be the first to volunteer to help out. She looked at Sarah's entranced face and smiled. She was pretty sure Sarah would want to come back if she knew it was to help injured baby animals.

'You girls should find Sophie. I know she wants to talk to you about the bushfires before your ride,' said Mark.

Poppy glanced at the others. They looked as concerned as she felt. On weekends Aunt Sophie usually let them choose what riding they wanted to do, but maybe she was going to tell them it was too dangerous to trail ride.

When they'd all taken a turn feeding the babies, they headed towards the stables. Casper came bounding out of nowhere and they all dropped down to greet him. Sarah laughed and hugged him as he licked her face. She was much more comfortable around dogs than horses, Poppy couldn't help noticing.

'There you are!' Aunt Sophie called out, emerging from the stables. She walked quickly towards them, brushing her hands against her jods. Sarah stood up and Aunt Sophie slung an arm around her shoulders. 'How's the new recruit?'

Sarah pulled a face. 'Can I be the new baby animal recruit rather than the riding recruit?' she said in a jokey way, although Poppy suspected she wasn't kidding.

Aunt Sophie laughed and shook her head. 'The girls have been so excited about you coming this weekend. We'll make a rider out of you yet.'

'That's what I hoped you *wouldn't* say.'

Aunt Sophie gave Sarah a squeeze, before going all serious, and Poppy knew she was going to give them the lowdown on the fires. Sarah dropped to her knee again, patting Casper as he lay on his back for a tummy tickle, loving the attention.

'Girls, as I'm sure you're all aware, there have been some very big bushfires over the past month, and I just want to make sure you understand the seriousness of any situation involving fire.'

Aunt Sophie leaned against the post and rail fence, looking at each of them. 'I don't want to scare you, but it's something we need to talk about before you go riding.'

They were all silent and Poppy never took her eyes off her aunt. Fire terrified her, especially when there were animals involved. It was amazing that her uncle was helping out, but she'd seen the news on TV before her mum had switched it off. There were pictures of charred black trees, and the newsreader said many animals hadn't survived. She'd heard that people died trying to save their homes too. It had been one of the worst-ever seasons for fire.

'They haven't been close to here, have they?' Katie asked, her voice way more timid than usual.

'Not too close,' Aunt Sophie replied, 'and we're lucky that the weather hasn't been as hot this past week, but we still need to be vigilant. I'll take you for a walk after your ride to show you our plans for the horses if we receive any warnings, but I want you all to be careful. It's very dry and even a tractor working a field and getting too hot could ignite something. So stay safe, don't ride anywhere without telling me, keep a mobile phone on you at all times, and if you see fire . . .'

Poppy gulped. 'We get home. Fast.'

Aunt Sophie nodded. 'Just be sensible, that's all. Okay?'

Poppy nodded. 'Okay.'

'Sure thing, Mrs D,' Milly said.

Sarah looked worried and Poppy grabbed her hand and squeezed it. 'It's just a precaution,' she assured her.

Sarah smiled back, but Poppy could tell she was freaked out, probably as much from the fire danger as the idea of horse riding. Poppy sighed. Just another reason for Sarah not to come back to Starlight Stables. Things really weren't going quite to plan.

CHAPTER THREE

Back in the Saddle

Milly and Katie were busy chatting now that they'd brought the ponies in, and Poppy was half-listening to them talk about school as she checked Crystal's girth to make sure it was tight enough. The last thing she wanted was to put her foot in the stirrup to get on and end up with her saddle under her pony's tummy! It seemed fine, and she quietly let herself out of Crystal's stable for a moment to check on Sarah. She'd left her alone for a bit while she got Crystal ready.

'Have you been talking to Missy?' Poppy asked Sarah when she crossed over to the stall Sarah was standing outside of. She'd wanted to show Sarah how to do everything but her friend had decided to stand outside Missy's stable and get to know her pony instead.

Missy was one of Poppy's all-time favourite ponies at Starlight. She'd learnt to ride on Missy as a complete beginner when she was seven years old, and even though she was too tall to ride her now, she sometimes still took the little grey out for a short ride. Sarah was lucky she wasn't tall, otherwise she'd have had to go onto a bigger horse, which would have been way more scary.

'No.' Sarah looked confused. 'What am I supposed to say to a horse, anyway?'

Poppy found it hard to explain, because everything about horses and being around them felt so natural to her. She always talked to Crystal when she groomed her or saddled her up. It just seemed normal.

'I don't know ... tell her how pretty she is, or tell her the truth – that you're a little scared and you want her to go easy on you.'

Sarah gave her a half-smile. 'You *actually* talk to them? It wasn't just something you told me to do for my nerves?'

Poppy shook her head and let herself into the stall.

'Missy is the kindest, sweetest pony in the world,' she told Sarah. She stroked Missy's muzzle, blowing on her nostrils softly. Horses always loved that, and Missy was no exception. 'I rode her for years, every time I came here, and the only time I ever fell off was riding her bareback. She's the perfect beginner pony.' Poppy laughed at the memory. 'We were trotting and I tried to jump her with her cover on, just holding the lead rope as makeshift reins. She stopped and put her head down to eat grass, and I sailed straight over the jump without her!'

Poppy was still laughing when she realised Sarah was squirming nervously on the spot and had wrapped her arms around herself tightly.

'I don't think I can do it,' Sarah whispered. 'I know it will sound crazy to you, but I'm kind of scared!'

'Do what?' Milly suddenly appeared, her trademark big smile planted on her face. She had her helmet sandwiched between her legs while she tried to tame her dark curls into a low ponytail.

'Sarah hasn't ridden before,' Poppy explained.

'Oh,' said Milly, rolling her eyes. 'You'll be fine. Just get on and we'll help you.'

Sarah gave Poppy a desperate look, and Poppy felt like thumping Milly on the arm. She was so rude sometimes!

'How about we lead Missy out, and then you can stand with her and watch us have a lesson,' Poppy quickly suggested.

Sarah nodded. 'Okay.'

Poppy gave Milly a stern look, hoping she'd realise that she didn't want to scare off Sarah by pushing her too hard on the first day. 'Just let me go and get her saddle. I'll be right back,' Poppy said.

Milly followed her and Poppy moved in close. 'She's not that keen.'

'I know, weird huh?'

Poppy sighed. 'I guess not everybody loves horses as much as we do. You need to be a bit more sensitive.'

'Yeah, I can tell she doesn't love them,' Milly said with a giggle, head bent close to Poppy's. 'I just don't know why you bothered to bring her here?'

Poppy gave her a soft play punch in the arm and Milly howled like it really hurt. Then she looked past Milly and went bright red.

Poppy spun around. Sarah was standing in the door and she looked upset. Poppy's heart sunk. How much had she heard? Before she could say anything there was a thump-thump of boots on concrete and Katie was suddenly right behind them.

'Hey, I've been thinking,' Katie said, breathing heavily and totally unaware of what had just happened. 'Why don't we take Sarah for a nice long trail ride, just walking. You could lead her from Crystal if it would make her feel safer? She needs to have a really nice first ride.'

Katie smiled at Sarah and Sarah smiled weakly back. Poppy wished she could wind back time and yell at Milly for being so insensitive.

'Perfect idea,' Poppy said, trying to forget what had happened. She was annoyed she hadn't thought of it herself. The only problem would be getting Sarah into the saddle in the first place. She hadn't really had a plan for getting Sarah to ride, she'd just hoped that once she spent time with Aunt Sophie instructing her, she'd discover how fun it was. Now she was realising it may not be that easy.

Poppy hauled Missy's saddle down and started

to lug it to the stables. Casper's wagging tail caught her eye. He was frozen in position, staring at a pile of horse rugs.

'Casper, what are you doing?' she asked.

He glanced back at her then stared at the rugs again, growling, head bent low.

'Hey guys, Casper thinks he's found a mouse,' said Poppy. At least, I hope it's a mouse and not a snake, she suddenly thought to herself.

Milly and Katie went dead still. They were obviously thinking the same thing.

'What is it?' Milly asked, nervously.

It was Sarah who moved first, shuffling over to Casper and bending low, slinging her arm around the Australian shepherd's neck. She didn't seem to be scared at all.

'Be careful,' Poppy cautioned, just as a streak of something black and furry leapt out. Milly shrieked and Poppy jumped.

They all breathed a sigh of relief when they saw that it was a tiny kitten hissing at them with his back arched, chest puffed up like a little lion.

Casper let out a loud woof, tail wagging now.

'Shhh,' Poppy scolded him.

'It's so cute!' Sarah exclaimed.

The kitten hissed loudly in reply and backed further into the corner of the stable.

'Do you think we'll be able to catch it?' Sarah asked, standing slowly, one hand still on Casper's head.

Poppy rested the saddle on her hip. 'No way. She's wild. We can put food out and she might get more relaxed around us eventually, but I doubt she'll ever be tame.'

Sarah looked sad. 'So she just has to live alone?'

'No, she can live here,' Poppy said. 'They've had a barn cat before, one that Uncle Mark found living in the hay barn.' Even though she was trying to sound casual, it made her upset to meet another animal without its parents.

Everyone stood there, staring at the kitten, and Casper kept wagging his tail like he'd just found something exciting to play with and wasn't about to let it go.

'Casper, leave,' Poppy instructed. '*Leave,*' she said in a slightly louder voice this time, making sure he knew she was serious. She watched as he turned and slowly walked away, whining softly.

'What's going on in here?' Aunt Sophie's voice carried through the barn and into the tack room.

'Casper found a kitten,' called Poppy.

Aunt Sophie laughed, leaning in the doorway, her black riding boots crossed at the ankle. 'That's Ghost. I forgot to tell you about him.'

'He's yours?' Sarah asked.

'Well, as ours as a wild cat ever will be,' Aunt Sophie said, entering the room. 'We're a sucker for unloved animals and this one had a burnt paw when we found him, so Mark has built him a nice little nesting box full of hay to sleep in. Don't worry about him, he's all hiss and no bite, although he did give Mark a sharp nip when he was tending his leg!'

Poppy noticed Milly nervously sliding behind Sarah, wide eyes locked on the kitten.

'Don't tell me that big brave Milly is scared of an itty bitty kitty cat?' Poppy asked, grinning.

Sarah giggled, then clamped a hand over her mouth.

'Can we just go ride horses?' Milly moaned, still hiding behind Sarah. 'I haven't been in the saddle for almost two weeks!'

'Go warm up your horses, girls. I'll take that from

you, Poppy, and saddle up Missy. Sarah and I will be out in a bit,' Aunt Sophie said. 'Come on, Sarah, I'll show you what to do. I'll teach you anything and everything you need to know when you're ready.'

'Um. I thought I'd just watch for a while,' said Sarah, hopefully.

'No problem. Let's get these girls out there riding and you can see what you think. Poppy's already told me you're not obsessed with horses like she is, so we'll just take it slow.' Aunt Sophie passed Sarah the bridle she'd been carrying, and flashed her a kind smile. 'How about we start with you watching me put her gear on. If you don't feel like riding, no one's going to pressure you. But it'd be nice for the option to be there if you change your mind.'

Poppy watched Sarah visibly relax and smiled her thanks at her aunt, then she turned and raced to Crystal's stable. She was desperate to spend some time with her pony. She only got to be with her every second weekend and holidays, so she didn't like missing even one minute of grooming her, riding her, or just being around her. But she was definitely going to apologise to Sarah as soon as she got her alone – she didn't want her to think they'd been laughing about her behind her back.

'You ready?' Katie called out from her stable as Poppy was slipping the bit into Crystal's mouth. Poppy quickly secured the leather bridle over Crystal's ears, checking her mane wasn't stuck beneath it, and then did the throat lash up.

'Yup. Give me one sec,' she called back. That was all it took for her to do up the noseband, then she was collecting her helmet from the hook and leading Crystal out.

They led the horses through the barn and past the other stables. Poppy could hear Aunt Sophie's soft laughter and reassuring words from Missy's stable, but she didn't wait. Instead, she followed her friends out into the bright summer sunshine. She put the reins over Crystal's head, gathered up her reins and slipped her left foot into the stirrup, swinging up and landing softly in the saddle. She slipped her other foot into the stirrup now she was seated, gave Crystal a pat on the neck and straightened up.

'Ready to roll?' Milly asked.

Poppy gave Milly a silly salute. 'Yes, sir,' she said, which sent them into peals of laughter. Poppy felt instantly happy when she was sitting in the saddle, riding her own pony. She stopped laughing, but the smile stayed glued to her face.

The three girls rode side by side towards the arena, knees bumping every now and again as they walked. Crystal had her ears pricked forward, walking fast, eager to get going. Poppy sighed with content. Nothing beat getting back in the saddle again. She gave Crystal another pat on the neck, looking around at the blue gum branches waving softly in the breeze, the parched yellow grass that stretched as far as her eyes could see. Starlight Stables was the most special place in the world to her, and she'd do anything to make Sarah love it, too. But what if she didn't? And was Milly right? Would Poppy have to choose between them?

'Anyone feel like jumping today?' Aunt Sophie asked, standing in the centre of the arena.

'Yes!' Poppy cried, a heartbeat ahead of Milly and Katie. She loved doing the arena work, but jumping was her absolute favourite. She glanced over at Sarah and gave her a quick wave.

'I want you all to exit the arena at a walk and head to the first cross-country jump. Milly, you're up first since you and Joe did the best canter today during our dressage training, then Poppy and Katie.'

Poppy gathered up her reins and headed toward the exit after Milly. Once they were out they rode side by side, their horses walking fast because they knew exactly where they were heading. Crystal loved to jump as much as Poppy did, and she always started a little jig-jog that made it hard for Poppy to sit deep in the saddle without bouncing along.

Aunt Sophie's cross-country jumping course was amazing, even better than riding in the show-jumping arena. This was where they were allowed to go fast in a gallop across the grass, slowing only as they approached each sturdy jump. The show-jumping rails always fell easily if a horse knocked them, but these cross-country jumps were made from timber and brush and other permanent materials, which meant they always felt more dangerous to train over. But Poppy wanted to be an eventing rider, and that meant she had to master all three phases – dressage, show jumping and cross-country.

She glanced over her shoulder and saw that Aunt Sophie was leading Missy, and Sarah was walking close beside her rather than on the other side of the sweet little grey. She sighed. It was harder having Sarah here than she'd thought, because it was difficult to concentrate on riding when she was worried about her friend not having a good time.

'I'm ready!' Milly called out.

'Off you go then,' Aunt Sophie called back.

Poppy halted Crystal and Katie rode up beside her. 'Did you know the water jump actually has some water in it now?' Poppy said.

'No way.' Katie giggled and pointed her whip in Milly's direction. 'Did you tell Milly that?'

Poppy bit her lip, feeling guilty.

Katie traded glances with her. 'Joe's always so naughty whenever we ride through water. I hope Milly doesn't fall off.'

Poppy watched as Milly's chestnut pony soared over a jump covered in branches. Joe was so eager, bursting into a gallop the second he landed and heading straight for the next jump. She knew they would disappear from sight now for two jumps, and then the next was the bank, where Milly would go straight down into the water and then have to do a solid log jump back out onto the grass.

Joe appeared again, slowing down in preparation for the bank and the water drop. Poppy cringed, expecting to hear a cry from Milly when they dropped into actual water, but was surprised when Joe only hesitated for a few seconds before leaping back out of the water on the other side. He had two more jumps to go, and it was only a minute or so later that they were slowing to a canter, then a trot, and halting nearby.

'What's the big deal about jumping through water?' Sarah asked.

Poppy spun in her saddle to look down at Sarah, who was standing beside her. She felt bad for not explaining it to her before. 'Lots of horses freak when they see the water and they don't want to jump down into it. It's pretty cool though if they do.'

'Fantastic work, Milly!' Aunt Sophie enthused, putting Missy's reins over the pony's neck and leaving her standing beside Sarah as she walked over to Milly.

'Ah, a little warning about the water would have

been nice, Mrs D!' cried Milly.

'Milly, if I didn't keep you on your toes, who would? And I do want you girls to approach every course as if it's your first time riding it, because you never know what has changed or what might surprise your horse.'

They all laughed at Milly when she made an upset-sounding snort. But she didn't look cross for long, soon laughing along with them. Poppy quickly lifted her right leg forward and shortened her right stirrup by two holes, then did the same with her left, to get them the correct length for jumping.

'Milly, walk Joe until he stops blowing. Maybe you girls could all go for a trail ride once we're finished up here.'

'Can I go now?' Poppy asked as Crystal started to dance on the spot, as if she knew instinctively that it was her turn.

'Go for it,' Aunt Sophie replied.

Poppy nudged Crystal with her heels, wanting her to walk on, but instead she burst into a trot, and less than three strides later they were cantering. She rose in the saddle, heels planted firmly down as they covered the ground fast. Poppy kept her hands steady, reins short, as Crystal fought for her head, wanting to gallop. They approached the first jump and Poppy checked Crystal, asked her to slow down a few strides out, then they were soaring, flying over the first solid fence.

'Good girl!' Poppy praised, rising out of the saddle again, balancing steadily as they cantered fast.

Crystal loved the encouragement and they raced fast toward the next jump. Poppy's heart was beating quickly and she was breathing hard, excited and eager. They soared over the next one, then the next, heading out of sight past some low-lying trees. Once they'd cleared the double she headed back towards the water jump.

'Come on, girl, we can do it,' she said, taking her fingers off the reins on one side and giving Crystal a quick pat on the neck. She slowed her down as they approached the bank, asking her to trot. When they reached the top, Poppy put her legs firmly against Crystal's sides, pushing her on, and Crystal only hesitated for a second before dropping down. Poppy leaned back and loosened her reins so Crystal could use her neck properly, and they landed with a splash into the water. Four strides later they were making a clean jump over the log and heading towards home.

Poppy couldn't wipe the smile off her face when her friends came into view, but it was Aunt Sophie she was watching. Her aunt grinned proudly back at her and Poppy felt amazing

'Great round, Pops!' Aunt Sophie called out as she slowed to a walk.

'Good luck, Katie,' Poppy said as her friend cantered past. Poppy kept moving, knowing her aunt would want Crystal to be cooled down properly. Besides, Poppy wasn't ready to get off just yet. She loved jumping and every time she practised cross-country on Crystal it filled her with hope that she wasn't just dreaming about being on the Australian Young Rider Squad one day. If she trained hard enough and listened to Aunt Sophie every step of the way . . . she gulped and let the reins through her fingers until she was only holding the buckle.

Maybe she would get there. Maybe she could actually be the next Lucinda Fredericks or Megan Jones, or her all-time idol from New Zealand, five-time Burghley Horse Trials winner Andrew Nicholson.

She jumped off Crystal and threw her arms around her neck, hugging her tight. She had the best pony in the world to start on, and as far as she was concerned nothing could stop her.

Poppy looked over and saw Sarah waving, a big smile on her face.

'Hey!' Poppy called out, leading Crystal over to her.

'You did great, right?' Sarah grinned. 'I'm seriously impressed!'

'I loved it.' Poppy smiled. 'Crystal's pretty awesome, isn't she? You okay?'

'I'm fine. It's nice finally seeing you ride, and I've been looking at the trees to see if I can spot a koala.'

Poppy leaned against Crystal as Sarah tenderly stroked Missy's neck. She knew exactly where they might find a koala, and she couldn't wait to show Sarah. But first she had something to say.

'I'm really sorry you heard what Milly said about you being here.'

Sarah shrugged, but Poppy knew she was hurt. 'It's fine,' she murmered, looking away. 'But if you'd rather me leave. I mean . . .'

'No!' Poppy hated being torn between her friends. 'No way. I want you here, and if Milly says anything else mean then she'll have me to deal with.'

Sarah looked uncomfortable. 'So you don't think I don't belong here?'

Poppy shook her head. 'I wish you loved horses like I do, but no, I think you belong just fine.'

'So I just have to make friends with Milly and convince her I'm normal, huh?'

Poppy laughed. 'Leave Milly to me.'

CHAPTER FOUR

Sarah's First Ride

While Katie was walking Cody to cool him down, Aunt Sophie headed over to where Poppy, Milly and Sarah were standing with their ponies. Poppy had a feeling now was the time Aunt Sophie planned to get Sarah on a horse. She passed Milly her reins so she could help.

'What I'd like is to get you up onto Missy, and then take you for a nice little walk around on the lead,' Aunt Sophie said to Sarah gently. 'I'll be right beside you every step of the way, and I'll keep my hand on your leg until you're ready for me to let go.'

Sarah glanced at Poppy, and Poppy gave her an

encouraging smile. 'You'll be fine. Missy is used to teaching beginners, and I can walk on the other side if it makes you feel safer. Besides, she's so nice and small.'

Sarah let out a big sigh, and Poppy knew that she was about to say 'yes'. Whenever she wanted her friend to do something she just had to pester her over and over, and eventually she'd sigh and give in, just like when she'd agreed to come to Starlight in the first place. Poppy crossed her fingers behind her back.

'Fine,' Sarah said. 'But don't go laughing at me if I fall straight off the other side.'

Milly smirked and Poppy frowned at her. While Sarah secured her helmet, Aunt Sophie quickly stepped in and checked Missy's girth, before throwing the reins over her neck and clipping on a lead rope that she'd been carrying. Poppy stepped up to hold the rope while Aunt Sophie guided Sarah up onto the pony's back.

'You feeling okay?' Aunt Sophie asked.

Sarah looked nervous, but she reached for the reins and let Aunt Sophie put her feet in the stirrups. 'I'm okay. The ground's just a long way away.'

'Hey,' Aunt Sophie said with a laugh, 'I think that all the time! You should see how far the ground is from Jupiter.' Aunt Sophie's horse was a whopping 17.2 hands high, but although he was huge Poppy doubted her aunt ever worried about how far away the ground was.

'I want you to sit up nice and straight, shoulders back, chin up, eyes forward.'

They were familiar instructions to Poppy – not only had her aunt told her the exact same things when she was learning, but she'd heard her use those words to every new rider she taught.

'You're a natural,' Poppy told her friend happily as she walked along beside her. She touched Missy's neck, loving how soft the grey pony's hair felt beneath her fingers. She was all cute and cuddly like a teddy bear, and Poppy had spent plenty of time snuggling her when she'd first started coming to Starlight.

'It's actually not as bad as I thought it would be,' Sarah said as she rode.

'Told you,' Poppy said, ready to burst she was so excited that her friend was actually, *finally*, on a horse.

'I didn't say I liked it, just that it wasn't bad.'

Poppy rolled her eyes and pulled a silly face, which made Sarah laugh.

'Okay, now that you're up there, let's halt and I'll show you how to hold the reins properly,' Aunt Sophie instructed. 'When we ask for a halt, we sit up straight, squeeze our butt and sit deep in the saddle, with a light pressure on the reins, hands closed.'

Of course, Aunt Sophie was the one making Missy stop this time, but she was teaching Sarah how to do it if she was riding on her own. She went on to show Sarah how to hold the reins properly with her thumb on top, and Poppy stayed put when they walked off. Once she'd watched them walk around for a few minutes she went back to stand with Milly.

'She looks good,' Katie said as she approached them from behind.

Poppy nodded. 'I just can't believe she's actually sitting on a horse.'

Milly silently passed her Crystal's reins, but Poppy could see she was bursting to say something and it wasn't like Milly to hold back when she had an opinion.

'What is it?' Poppy asked.

Milly made a face, then collapsed dramatically over her pony's neck, arms looped around him. 'I know this sounds bad, but I just don't get how you and Sarah can be best friends if she doesn't even like horses a little bit.'

'Milly!' Katie scolded.

'What? It's true! Don't tell me you weren't thinking the exact same thing.'

Poppy leaned against Crystal, eyes trained on Sarah and Missy. Aunt Sophie had her twenty-foot rope extended now so that Sarah was being lunged in a small circle, still just walking, but learning properly.

'It's all right, I know what you mean,' she told Milly. 'I guess, where I grew up, none of my friends have ever been that into horses. It was always just me who was lucky enough to have an aunt with stables. And before Crystal, I only ever came here in the holidays.'

'It's just kind of crazy when you are completely obsessed with horses.'

Katie reached over and slapped Milly's helmet with her whip. 'Don't be mean to Poppy.'

'I'm not being mean!' Milly scowled. 'You're the one whacking me!' They didn't usually carry whips for their ponies, but the last time they'd been riding Aunt Sophie had told them to practise holding them sometimes when they were riding.

'I guess at home it doesn't matter. We have heaps of fun and she lets me harp on about horses anyway.' Poppy laughed. 'I spend so much time at her house, it's so cool; her mum makes the most amazing noodles and dumplings.'

'She seems really nice,' Katie said. 'And I'll bet she ends up loving riding once she gets the hang of it.'

'She is. She's super nice,' Poppy said, wanting to defend Sarah. It was tough sometimes because she didn't love horses, but she was still her best friend. 'We met when her family moved to Melbourne, when we were like six. She's been my best friend ever since.'

'Is she Chinese?' Milly asked.

'Duh.' Katie hit Milly with her whip again and Poppy tried to flick her with her reins, which made Milly howl and leap out of the way, alarming a sleepy-looking Joe.

'Yes. Why?'

'I dunno, just wondering if it's a Chinese thing, not liking horses. But she seems cool. I don't *want* to not like her.'

Poppy cracked up. She was pretty sure there were millions of Chinese girls who loved horses. It annoyed her that Milly thought it was weird to be friends with someone just because they didn't like horses. She'd never have thought about it like that. Sarah was Sarah. They'd been best friends since forever, and nothing was going to change that. If Sarah discovered that she liked riding, then Poppy'd be over the moon. But if she didn't, so what?

'That was kind of cool,' Sarah announced when she joined them, a grin on her face that made Poppy's heart leap. She couldn't believe Sarah was actually smiling when earlier she'd just about been in tears over the *idea* of riding.

'But of course! Horses are, like, the best things EVER!' Milly said.

'I knew you'd love it!' Poppy laughed.

'I wouldn't say that I loved it, but it wasn't that

bad. Once I got used to the movement.'

Poppy met Aunt Sophie's gaze, and she could tell that her aunt was pleased with how everything was going, too. It must have been strange for her, teaching Sarah. The kids who came to Starlight for riding lessons loved horses and were desperate to learn.

'I mentioned to Sarah that you might like to take her for a look around the farm on horseback. Perhaps do a short trail, just at a walk.'

'Sure thing,' Poppy agreed. 'I'll lead her and we can go really slow.'

'Sounds good,' Katie agreed.

'We might even have Sarah jumping by the time we get back!' Milly announced dramatically.

Poppy rolled her eyes. Milly was always over-enthusiastic, and it seemed that getting Sarah to learn everything about horse-riding in a couple of hours was her next harebrained idea.

'The only jumping I'll be doing is off this horse!' Sarah replied.

Poppy gave her what she hoped was a reassuring smile. 'Don't listen to Milly,' she said as Milly started to ride away. 'We all know she's kind of cuckoo.' Poppy made a face and twirled her finger in circles around her ear.

'I can hear you. You do know that, right?' Milly called out.

Poppy just laughed, holding up her hand for a high-five with Katie.

'So you're okay about going on a trail ride with us?' Poppy asked in a low voice so only Sarah could hear. Poppy absently stroked Missy's soft neck as she looked up at Sarah.

'Does that mean riding *on* a trail?'

Poppy smiled and nodded. 'Yep. We go for a nice ride through the bush, and we might even see some koalas out there. It'll be cool.'

Sarah shrugged. 'If you keep a very tight hold of me with this lead thing, I'll do it.'

'Lead rope,' Poppy corrected. 'And I promise not to let you go. We'll ride side by side the whole way and I'll be in control of Missy because I'll have hold of her. But she's always perfectly behaved, so you don't have to worry.'

'I'll take your word for it.' Sarah laughed suddenly and Poppy looked up at her.

'What?'

'You're just so different here. So sure about everything.'

Poppy grinned. At home, Sarah was the confident one, the one who always knew what to do. 'It's because I actually know what I'm doing here, I guess.'

'It's cool,' Sarah said. 'I can see why you like coming here so much now that I've been able to watch you ride Crystal.'

Aunt Sophie had finished talking to the others and walked back over to hold Missy while Poppy mounted. Poppy settled into her saddle and kept her stirrups short, preferring them at jumping length when she was hacking out. Not that they'd be cantering or jumping today, but still. It just felt more comfortable.

'So which way are we headed?' Sarah asked.

'That way,' Poppy replied, pointing off into the distance, past the arena. She was going to take her on a nice easy trail. 'It'll take maybe ten minutes walking before we enter the bush.'

'Listen up, everyone,' Aunt Sophie suddenly said. 'I want you all to remember what I said about fire today. Stay alert and be safe. I want you to enjoy yourselves just like normal, but be careful.'

Poppy traded glances with Katie. Her friend's eyes were as big as saucers.

'I'm being overly cautious, girls – the fires aren't in this area – but you're my responsibility while you're here, all of you, and so there is nothing wrong with a quick recap about safety. Okay?'

'We'll be careful, we promise,' Poppy said solemnly.

'I always have my phone on me,' Katie chimed in, patting the belt with her phone attached to it.

'Good. Me, too. So call me if *anything* happens. And nothing crazy, Milly,' Aunt Sophie warned. 'I don't need any heroes if we do have a fire situation; I just need you all safe.'

Milly blushed and nodded, and Poppy knew that no matter how fun and wild her friend could be, there was no way she'd be silly if it actually came to something as dangerous as a bushfire.

'Anyone else thinking that we should just flag the trail ride and stay home?' Sarah asked in a small voice.

Poppy laughed it off, although she could tell her aunt's seriousness had shaken them all. 'Don't be silly. The fires are in the next valley – not around here. Aunt Sophie is just being overly cautious. We'll be fine, right, Sophie?'

Her aunt patted her knee before stepping back. 'Absolutely. If I didn't believe that, then I wouldn't be letting you out of my sight. And I'd definitely be getting all the horses to a safer location.'

The girls set off in silence. Poppy fell deep into thought, imagining what would happen to Crystal if the fires reached Starlight Stables. She shook her head, trying to make the thoughts disappear.

'I've got goosebumps,' Milly said, making Poppy look up. Milly and Katie edged forward to ride side by side in front of Poppy and Sarah as they approached the trail leading into the bush and the path narrowed. Poppy tightened her grip around Missy's lead rope and smiled at Sarah.

'You're doing great,' she whispered quickly. 'I can't believe how good you look up there! You're a natural.'

'What if these guys got hurt?' Milly leaned down and flung her arms around Joe, her chest pressed against his chestnut neck as she hugged him. 'I love him so much.'

Katie ran her fingers down Cody's neck, and Poppy instinctively stroked Crystal's neck with the back of her knuckles. Out the corner of her eye, she saw Sarah's hand pat Missy, too, and she smiled to herself. Missy might succeed in winning Sarah over after all.

They were surrounded by bush now and it was so peaceful, except for the sound of creaking leather and the occasional birdsong. The girls chatted quietly about school and feeding the animals with Mark, and she relaxed as Sarah started to laugh and open up. They had been riding for almost half an hour when Katie stopped and pointed up into the tree canopy high over their heads.

'Hey, look up there!' she cried excitedly.

Poppy halted behind her, looking up into the trees and trying to see what she was pointing at.

'Poppy! Look! There's a koala!' Sarah exclaimed. She was grinning like mad, leaning back to get a better view as if she'd totally forgotten she was sitting on a horse.

'No way!' replied Poppy, placing a hand on Crystal's bottom and tipping back to get a better look. It was exactly what she'd *wanted* Sarah to see. If everything kept playing its part as well as this, maybe she'd get Sarah back here after all. 'I haven't seen any this close to the edge of the bush for ages.' The koala was directly above them, not moving except for the slow chew of its mouth as it ate a leaf. Poppy loved the wildlife around the farm; the towering blue gum trees that were home to the koala, the low-hanging branches near the creek where the kangaroos often relaxed in the shade. It felt like a special place, and she felt special because she got to see it all and ride among it – she hoped Sarah was feeling some of that specialness, too.

'Oh! Is that a . . .' Sarah's voice trailed off for a second. 'Yes! It's a baby, on her back. See it peering over her head now?'

Poppy clamped her hand over her mouth, unable to believe her eyes. Sarah was right – there was a baby on her back, almost camouflaged against its mum because they were the exact same shade of grey.

'That's amazing,' Milly whispered. 'They look so cute!'

Poppy laughed. They *did* look cute, but she'd never forget Uncle Mark's description of them.

'Cute outfit, nasty surprise,' he'd told her.

'Uncle Mark says their claws are crazy sharp and you should never try to touch them,' Poppy said. 'He said that just because they look like cuddly bears doesn't mean they are.'

The girls all sat in silence a while longer, watching the koala. Her baby was almost invisible half the time because she was tight to her mum's back, only peering over between her ears every now and then.

'You were right about this place,' Sarah said. 'It is pretty amazing.'

Poppy looked over at her friend, smiling. 'I knew you'd love it if you gave it a chance.'

'I'm not crazy about horses, but it is really special coming here. Thanks for making me.'

'Thanks for coming!' Poppy grinned. She'd been begging Sarah for years to come with her. It wasn't until she had started talking non-stop about Milly and Katie that she'd finally been able to convince her. If only she'd told her about all the other cool stuff at Starlight, she bet Sarah would have come sooner.

'Want to keep going?' Milly called out from the

front, already moving on. She was often the leader because Joe always liked to be in front, the little part Arab pony was used to stepping out and keeping his nose just in front of the others.

Poppy nudged her pony back into a walk. 'You okay?' she asked Sarah as they headed off again.

Sarah was still staring back at the koala and its baby as she gathered up her reins. 'Yep, fine.'

'You sure you don't want to try trotting?' Milly called back. 'Or cantering or jumping?'

Sarah looked shocked, so Poppy answered for her. 'Yeah, she's sure. Besides, the horses have already had a big workout this morning.'

'Yeah, I know,' Milly grumbled. She was never content with going slow.

'Where did you ride onto that guy's land?' Sarah asked, her voice carrying loud and clear.

'Oh, just up through there,' Milly replied, pointing to where the bush thinned and you could glimpse paddocks stretching away. 'We jumped an old rickety gate and raced to the barn. It was crazy cool.'

At the time Poppy knew they'd all been terrified, but it was fun thinking back. She looked around, imagined seeing the farm and bush arrounding Starlight Stables for the first time. Sarah had a much bigger house than the one Poppy shared with her mum and brother, but even though it was large, there was only a small lawn outside. Poppy didn't mind living in the city because she got to come here so often – she had the best of both worlds – but Sarah was such a city girl, Poppy bet she'd never trekked through the bush like this and seen what it was like in the country.

The ground was cushioned in pine needles and the trees above gave them shade from the hot sun. In some places the branches crisscrossed, making it feel like an umbrella above them, and Poppy loved titling her head back and staring up, seeing the blue pockets of sky where the trees parted.

On the times she'd ridden with her aunt, she'd seen just about every type of animal, from birds and snakes to wombats and kangaroos. It was so amazing, and when she was older it was the type of place she wanted to live. Somewhere she could train horses and ride every day. Starlight had always been her favourite place in the world, and since her dad had died it was even more special – it was the only place she felt calm, and like she could really forget about everything else. Sarah was right – she was different here, and in a good way. Back at home and at school, she always felt a bit out of place. But here, she felt like she belonged. She knew what she was doing, and she was confident doing it because it was what she loved.

'How are you doing, Sarah?' Katie asked, jolting Poppy from her thoughts. 'Do you want to head back?'

'Already?' Milly groaned before Sarah could get any words out. 'We haven't got going properly yet.'

Poppy laughed. 'Yeah, let's head back. The horses will have had enough. Why don't we see if we can head out tomorrow for the whole day?'

'Yes! We could show Sarah the farm, ride right out to the boundary,' Milly suggested.

'Why don't we take a picnic? It could be really fun.' Katie was grinning and Poppy was pleased she'd suggested a ride out over the farm.

'Sounds like a plan. I'll ask Aunt Sophie when we get back.' Poppy paused and looked at Sarah. 'We might even be able to spot a kangaroo or two,' she told her, ready to say anything to get Sarah to agree to coming. If she liked this, she'd love riding out over the whole farm.

'Okay. So long as you keep that thingy attached to me.'

'The lead rope,' Poppy told her. 'And yes, I will.'

'Awesome. Let's get back and ask Mrs D,' Milly said, turning Joe and riding straight through the middle of Poppy and Sarah.

'Milly!' Poppy yelled, struggling to keep hold of the lead rope then losing it entirely when Joe didn't stop in time. Missy took a step back to get out of the way and Sarah almost lost her balance, sliding sideways and desperately clutching at Missy's mane.

Milly backed up her pony. Sarah looked wobbly as Poppy quickly dismounted and picked the rope up again, giving her friend what she hoped was a reassuring smile.

'Sorry,' Poppy muttered. 'Blame Milly, that was her fault.'

'Sorry,' Milly apologised, looking sheepish. 'I . . .'

'It's fine,' Sarah mumbled. 'Milly didn't mean to.'

Only Poppy knew it wasn't fine, and she didn't

know why Sarah was sticking up for Milly when they could all see that she was shaken up. She really wanted Sarah to enjoy herself. The last thing she wanted was for Sarah to feel too scared to get back on a horse, especially after she'd done so well today.

'Come on, let's go,' Poppy said, deciding it was better to change the topic. 'I bet Aunt Sophie will have something yummy for us for lunch, and we might be able to help out with another feed if Uncle Mark's in with the injured animals again.'

'He's so cool,' Sarah said as she rode beside them three-abreast now the trail was wider. Katie was riding just behind them. Unlike Joe, her lovely horse Cody wasn't at all worried about being last.

'You mean Mark?' Poppy asked. When Sarah nodded she grinned. 'He *is* pretty awesome.' It was so exciting that Sarah liked Mark's little wildlife centre.

'I would do anything for an uncle like that,' Milly agreed. 'He is definitely cool.'

Sarah and Milly grinned at each other and Poppy started to relax a bit.

'Me too,' Katie piped up. 'He's a vet, he owns this beautiful place and he rides horses. Everything about him is perfect.'

'He's mine, all mine!' Poppy declared dramatically. 'So hands off!'

The others laughed as they rode back towards the stables. Katie was absolutely right, mused Poppy. Mark was the perfect uncle, and Sophie was the perfect aunt. Having them had helped so much when she'd lost her dad, and she would never, ever be able to thank them enough for giving her Crystal. She'd wanted her own pony for years, from before she could even ride, and because of them her dream had come true.

CHAPTER FIVE

Prince

'How did I never know this was here?' Milly asked, her shoulder bumping Poppy's as they followed Aunt Sophie on foot.

Poppy was tired from the trail ride earlier in the day, but she was curious to see what her aunt had to show them. Poppy had always known there was a plan in place in case of fire, but she hadn't ever really thought about it that much. She gulped, imagining fire burning across the property.

'So you would bring all the horses here?' she asked, surveying the huge empty paddock. There were no trees and virtually no grass. It was like a huge dust bowl.

Aunt Sophie nodded and pointed to the gate at the far corner. 'It's really important to make sure the horses are contained, so we would bring them in through that gate there and ensure they're all locked in here. If we had time, we'd wet the entire area, but as it is there are no trees or vegetation nearby, so nothing to feed the fire, and we ensure this area stays completely grass-free now, other than the little creek running through the middle over there. And if you look around the fence line there is a one-metre break made from sand right around the perimeter to try to stop a fire from spreading, with a line of stones beyond that.'

'When did you do this?' Poppy asked.

'Mark has become more worried about fire this season, so we've slowly been getting it up to standard over the last month.'

Poppy felt goosebumps all over. She pushed up against Sarah and looped her arm through her friend's. The thought of having to leave Crystal in this safe area while a fire was raging was too terrifying a thought.

'And they'd be safe in here?'

She could tell from the look on Sophie's face

that she wasn't sure about that at all. Her aunt grimaced. 'It's the best we can do. We keep that big tub of water full at all times during summer. We'd take the horses' halters off, and of course none of them would be allowed to wear covers. It's not nice to think about, but we have to be prepared just in case we're stuck here with no other option.'

'What if they got out? If they jumped?' Katie asked.

Poppy glanced at her, watching as Katie wrapped her arms tight around herself.

'We do everything we can to keep them contained so they're not a danger to fire crews or other residents. If we had time, we'd truck as many horses as we could to a safe location, but fires are unpredictable. We're just lucky that we haven't had one here before.'

Poppy would bet anything that her aunt would get Jupiter out somehow – he was worth so much money and Sophie adored him. She'd had the big gelding since he was a baby. But she had to believe that Aunt Sophie would do whatever she could to save Crystal and the other ponies, too.

'Can we go now?' Milly asked, her voice way

quieter than it usually was. 'All this talk about fires is making me feel sad.'

'Sure,' Aunt Sophie said with a smile. 'I just wanted you girls to know our plan in the worst-case scenario, because I don't remember it ever being so dry here. One spark could be devastating for the area.' Poppy watched as she patted Milly's shoulder and then gave her a hug. Milly usually acted all brave and dare-devilish, but this time she looked as sombre as they all did. 'Besides, if we have advance warning, we'll be getting every single horse out of here. There's not one animal on this property that I want hurt, not if I can help it. I just need you girls to be in charge of your own pony if there is an emergency, because they know you and trust you, and this is where I want you to bring them.'

'Can we go help Mark now? I think we all need some baby animal cuddling,' Sarah said. She was obviously trying to change the mood, and Poppy smiled at her.

'Well, first I have something else to show you girls.'

Poppy's heart started to thud. 'What is it?' she asked.

'Is it a horse?' Milly asked excitedly. 'Another animal at the clinic? A puppy?'

'Follow me,' Aunt Sophie said mysteriously.

Poppy giggled, keeping hold of Sarah's arm as they raced off, having to slow down when they quickly overtook Aunt Sophie.

'It's another rider!' Milly suddenly burst out.

'Mils!' Katie yelled. 'Just let her tell us!'

Poppy traded glances with Sarah. It probably wasn't as exciting for her because she didn't love horses, but she still seemed happy to be part of the fun.

'It's a new horse,' Poppy whispered. 'I'll bet it is. Nothing else would put a smile like that on Sophie's face.'

Sarah shrugged. 'Whatever it is, she looks pretty happy about it.'

'A baby!' Milly shrieked. 'You've had a baby!'

'*Mils!*' This time it was Poppy. 'She didn't just pop out a baby!'

Katie rolled her eyes at Poppy. 'Yeah, and we somehow missed her big tummy?'

Milly's face fell, but Aunt Sophie started to laugh. 'You girls are terrible! There's no new puppy, and there's *definitely* no secret baby. I promise.'

'So what is it?' Milly asked, jumping up and down beside Aunt Sophie like she was about to burst from not knowing what was going on.

'Look,' Aunt Sophie said, her voice so low it was almost a whisper.

Poppy stopped at the same time as her friends. She'd been so absorbed in trying to figure out what it could be and listening to Milly's silly suggestions, that she'd hardly taken any notice of their surroundings. *And then she saw him.*

'Girls, I'd like you to meet Prince.'

Poppy gaped, her mouth hanging open. No one said a word as the beautiful, majestic-looking black horse trotted over to greet them, nostrils flared, mane flowing as he floated across the ground. He was one of the most incredible-looking animals Poppy had *ever* seen.

'He's amazing,' she whispered.

'Yeah, even I think he's gorgeous,' Sarah replied.

Aunt Sophie stepped forward, leaning over the gate and holding out her hand. The colt approached cautiously, snorting, his neck arched. 'He's my new baby.'

'Mrs D, he's . . .' Katie started, then stopped, clearly lost for words.

'The most beautiful creature in the world,' Milly announced, pushing past Poppy to get to him. Poppy nudged back, not about to let Milly get there first. She grinned when Milly pressed up against Aunt Sophie, poking out her tongue at Poppy. Poppy just rolled her eyes at Milly before staring at Prince. She couldn't take her eyes off the new horse.

'Did you get to name him?' Milly asked.

Aunt Sophie smiled. 'Yes. The stud we purchased him from never name their young stock. He's only rising two years old and they didn't do a lot with him except the basics, and aside from that he's just been turned out with their other youngsters. Now he's my new baby, and I thought it was the perfect name for him.'

'He sure looks like a Prince,' Sarah said from behind Poppy.

'Yeah, definitely the perfect name,' Milly said, sharing a smile with Sarah.

Poppy reached out a hand to touch his gleaming black neck. He pawed at the ground and stepped backward, turning fast on his haunches before cantering off down the paddock again. His trot had been magical, and his canter was just as incredible.

'Jupiter is getting older now, and even though I know he should have years left ahead of him, I want to have a young horse sitting quietly in the wings,' Aunt Sophie explained. 'Prince will be started under saddle as a three year old, then turned out to mature a bit longer, before I slowly start to train him.'

Poppy felt a pang for Jupiter, because the older gelding was used to having all Sophie's attention, but she knew he wouldn't be able to compete at the top level forever.

'Aunt Sophie, have you ever thought about what you'll do with Jupiter when you retire him?' Poppy asked, suddenly curious.

Her aunt turned. 'Why's that, Pop? I guess I haven't thought about it much.'

'It's just . . .' She wasn't sure how to say what she was thinking, mainly because she wasn't sure what she was trying to get across! And she almost didn't want to say it because she loved Crystal so much, but . . .

'Are you asking me if you could have him?' Aunt Sophie said gently, her voice low and soft.

Poppy's face burned hot, she could feel the blush straightaway. 'No! I mean, well, yes.' She buried her face in her hands, embarrassed. 'I mean, I love Crystal, don't get me wrong. But I would love to ride Jupiter when you've finished with him, once I'm older. I was just worried that you might be thinking of selling him.' She should have asked Aunt Sophie on her own, brought it up when it was just the two of them, and now she felt silly for even saying what she had. Of course her aunt wouldn't have thought about Poppy riding the amazing gelding one day – he was way too valuable and it would be years before Poppy would even be capable of taking him on! And just thinking about being too tall for Crystal upset her, even if it would be amazing to ride Jupiter one day.

'Poppy, if I decide to retire Jupiter from high-level competition when he's older, then of course I'd consider you riding him.'

Poppy's heart beat fast as she looked up and met Aunt Sophie's gaze. 'Really? You're not just saying that?'

'Of course I mean it,' she laughed. 'But hopefully that's years away, and I'm fortunate right now that

I'm in a position to own my own competition horse without having to have a partner. If I ever lost my sponsorship deals or things changed financially, then selling Jupiter could be a possibility.' She reached out for Poppy's hand and squeezed it. 'But that's so unlikely and it would break my heart even thinking about it, so don't go getting worried, okay?'

'Okay.' Poppy nodded, still staring at her aunt. All she could think about was that one day, *maybe*, she could be learning dressage on a horse that had qualified for the Olympics and the World Dressage Champs. One of *the* best horses in the country. It only made her all the more determined to learn everything she could and become the best rider she could be. She might want to be an event rider, but if she had the chance to ride Jupiter and learn dressage, then that's exactly what she would do.

'Can we go in with him?' Milly asked, her voice jolting Poppy from her thoughts. Her friend was leaning right over the top rail of the fence, looking desperate to get up close and personal with the young colt.

'He's only been here a few days and I don't know him well enough to trust him around you girls yet.

How about we just admire him from this side of the fence to start with.'

'Okay,' Milly grumbled, sounding like it was far from okay.

Katie had climbed up next to Milly, and the two of them continued to stare obsessively at Prince. Poppy glanced at Sarah, hoping her friend wasn't finding it all too boring, and realised Sarah had dropped to her knees and was rubbing Casper's belly. The dog must have snuck up behind them when Poppy was daydreaming about riding Jupiter.

'Girls, we have a few cattle that need to be checked on,' Aunt Sophie said, holding up her hand to shield her eyes from the bright sun. Poppy felt a trickle of sweat down her back and suddenly realised how hot it had become. 'Mark purchased two dozen yearling heifers, and it'd help us out big-time if you could ride out and check on them, make sure they don't have any visible injuries and check their water troughs. Could you do that for your ride tomorrow?'

'Sure thing,' Poppy replied.

'Yep, no problem, Mrs D,' Milly answered, still staring at Prince. Poppy followed her gaze and laughed when she saw him rear up at another horse in the paddock, pawing out with one of his front legs then landing back on all four hooves before cantering off.

'Will you be okay going riding again, Sarah?'

Poppy watched Sarah, crossing her fingers behind her back and hoping that she would say yes to Aunt Sophie's question. They'd had fun out trail riding even though they'd only been walking. Surely she'd want to ride again!

'Um, maybe,' Sarah replied.

'Maybe?' Poppy planted her hands on her hips. 'You have to say yes! Missy was so good for you and you were great and . . .'

'Fine!' Sarah laughed. 'I'll go. But walking only. There's no way I want to fall off and land on my bum.'

Milly giggled. 'That'd actually be pretty clever if you landed on your bum. Most people land on their head or get dragged behind the horse with their foot in the stirrup when they hit the ground for the first time,' she said.

Sarah went white.

'Milly!' Aunt Sophie scolded her before Poppy

could kick her. 'First of all, that's untrue, and second of all, it's downright mean to scare Sarah like that.'

Milly shrugged. 'Sorry.'

'Has anyone ever actually fallen off Missy?' Katie asked. 'She has to be one of the sweetest ponies here.'

Poppy bit the inside of her mouth to stop from smiling when she saw Aunt Sophie wink at Katie. She was secretly thanking her for turning the subject around.

'I don't remember it ever happening. That's why we use her for the learners.'

Sarah still looked unsure, but she eventually sighed and gave in. 'Okay. I'll do it. But if my legs *or* my butt hurt too bad, I'm changing my mind.'

'Yay!' Poppy threw her arms around Sarah and jumped up and down.

'Can we go and see if Mark needs a hand feeding the baby animals?' Sarah asked once the happy dance was over.

'Sure thing. You girls run on ahead. I'm going to spend a few minutes with Prince.'

Half of Poppy wanted to stay to watch her aunt

with the new horse, but the other half was bursting to run off with her friends and bottle feed the cute animals. She looked at Aunt Sophie, saw she was already focused on Prince, and decided to let her have some time alone with him. She grabbed Sarah's hand and they started to run.

'Wait up!' Katie called out.

'Poppy!' Milly yelled. 'Don't you dare get there first!'

But Poppy wasn't slowing down and Sarah was a fast runner. She glanced back and saw Milly's arms pumping as she tried to catch them, but it only made Poppy want to go faster. They might be her best friends in the world, but she still liked to beat them.

CHAPTER SIX

Ready for Adventure

'What do you think we should take?' Katie asked that night as she and Milly collapsed on their stretcher beds.

Poppy stretched out on her bed, staring up at the ceiling of the large bedroom. Sarah sat cross-legged at the other end. She was sharing the bed with Poppy so they could all be together in one room, and they were going top and tails. Poppy doubted Sarah would much like her feet in her face, but she hadn't complained yet, and it wasn't like they hadn't top and tailed a million times when they stayed at each other's houses.

'Your feet stink,' Sarah said, pushing her away

when Poppy flexed her toes.

'Do not,' Poppy muttered, pushing them further toward Sarah.

'Eww! They're like rotten eggs!'

Milly burst out laughing and Sarah joined in. Poppy reluctantly pulled her feet back and decided to find some socks, although she was secretly happy that Milly and Sarah were joking together.

'Are we going to be gone the whole day?' Katie asked, not even bothering to join in with the teasing.

Poppy had been thinking about the beautiful colt Prince, not about their next ride. It was almost impossible not to think about her aunt's new horse, imagining him floating around the arena doing dressage with Aunt Sophie schooling him. She wanted to make Crystal move like that, to teach her all the fancy dressage moves she'd seen her aunt ride.

'Pops?' Sarah said, nudging her in the side with her elbow. 'Your feet aren't that bad. Sorry.'

'Bet she was dreaming about Prince,' Milly said with a snort. 'Poor horse had better hope she doesn't ride barefoot!'

Poppy grinned at Milly, laughing off her silly jokes. 'Ha ha, but yes, I was.' She giggled. 'And

Crystal. I'm always dreaming about Crystal.'

'Prince was amazing,' Katie said.

'Better than amazing. He was just . . .'

Sarah laughed. 'Amazing,' she said, shaking her head. 'I get that he was beautiful to look at, but I don't get what you all go ga-ga over.'

'You're kidding, right?' Milly teased, rolling her eyes. 'Have you taught her *nothing* about horses, Poppy?'

Poppy leaned back on Sarah. 'Yeah, once you learn how to ride on your own, to canter and jump and do all the crazy fun stuff that makes you feel invincible, then you'll get it.'

'Imagine you're dreaming about being a princess riding a magical unicorn,' Katie said, her voice all dreamy. 'Because that's how it would feel riding a horse like Prince once he's trained by Mrs D.'

Sarah looked at them like they were crazy and they burst into giggles. Poppy was just happy that they were all laughing, that Sarah wasn't being left out.

'When I have a cool dream, I'm always flying. I don't think I've ever ridden a unicorn in my dreams,' Sarah told them when they'd stopped laughing.

'Oooh, that'd be fun,' Katie said.

'My cool dreams are always on horseback,' Poppy said. 'So maybe that's telling you something.'

'What, like she should strap on a pair of wings and learn how to fly?' Milly asked.

'I actually want to be a pilot when I grow up. All I've ever wanted is to go in a helicopter,' Sarah said in a quiet voice.

Poppy glanced at Sarah, giving her a quick smile. She knew what Sarah dreamed of being – whenever they had a sleepover at home, Sarah always woke up telling her about a flying dream, and Poppy was always telling her about her Crystal dreams.

'That's a really cool thing to want to be,' Katie said.

'Yeah, that sounds awesome actually,' Milly agreed reluctantly.

'Hey, so back to tomorrow,' Poppy said, thinking about the day ahead. 'Should we ride out early before it gets too hot? Or do you want to go in the afternoon?'

'We have to muck out all the stables and help feed out the other horses, so maybe we should do that early and head off straight after,' Katie suggested.

'Sounds like a plan,' Poppy agreed. 'We just need to tell Aunt Sophie that we're going to spend the whole day out riding.'

'Ugh, my legs are already killing me after riding for, like, an hour!' Sarah protested with a groan.

'I was thinking we could ride, find the cattle, then stop somewhere for lunch,' Poppy suggested. 'We could sit under a tree and eat, explore a bit, then ride back when we're ready. It'll be fun.'

'Cool, gets my vote,' Milly said, flopping back on her bed and landing with a squeak. 'Ow!'

Poppy laughed and wriggled past Sarah so she could get off the bed. The carpet was soft beneath her toes as she walked over to the light switch. 'Ready for sleep?' she asked.

'Yep,' Katie said at the same time as Milly muttered something that sounded like 'yes'.

She flicked the switch and jumped over Sarah to get back to her spot on the bed. It wasn't completely dark – the light from the hall sent a slither of brightness into their upstairs room through the half-closed door.

'Sweet dreams,' Poppy whispered. She wanted to stay awake for longer, chatting, but she was so tired. She shut her eyes and saw Crystal in her mind, the way she always leaned over for a cuddle, dropping her head to Poppy's shoulder, or how she tried so hard to learn new things when they were having a lesson.

Poppy loved riding Crystal, but one day when she was a grown-up she wanted to be just like her aunt. She wanted to follow in her footsteps and do something she loved, riding the best and most amazing horses. Sarah might want to be a pilot, and that sounded cool, but all Poppy wanted to do was ride. Especially when she saw her mum go off to work every day with a fake smile on her face like she was happy to be working in an office. Poppy knew she hated it, and she didn't want to grow up and spend the rest of her life doing something that she didn't like.

Poppy slurped down the last of her Milo and took one last bite of her Vegemite toast as her friends did the same.

'Do you want me to pack lunch for you?' Aunt Sophie asked as she loaded the dishwasher.

Katie stood to help her, collecting up all their plates. Poppy quickly gathered the glasses, not wanting her aunt to have to do too much for them. She knew how special it was that they were allowed to stay so often, and she always liked to help out whenever she could. Besides, it was nothing compared to what it had been like at home when her mum had a kind of breakdown after her dad died. Back then she'd had to do everything just to make it look like life was okay for her and her brother.

'We're fine, Mrs D,' Milly said. 'We can just grab an apple and a bag of chips or something.'

'How about I make lunch while you do your chores,' Sarah said. 'I don't mind, and I can help Mark – um, Mr D, I mean – if he needs an extra pair of hands while giving the little animals their breakfast.'

Poppy saw the pleading look in Sarah's eyes and guessed she didn't want to help out with the horses. Poppy was so used to doing chores, but she could see that they would be boring for someone who didn't like horses.

Milly looked up. She knew Sarah didn't want to

be around the ponies and doing all the horsey jobs. But before Milly could say anything, Aunt Sophie smiled.

'Good idea, Sarah. I don't want you going hungry if you're out riding. You need to keep your strength up. Make sure you take lots of sandwiches and not just snacks if you're staying out all day.'

'Yes, Ma'am,' Milly said, making Poppy giggle as she saluted behind Aunt Sophie.

Sophie suddenly spun round and flicked Milly with the tea towel she was holding. Milly squealed in shock, and they all roared with laughter.

'Off with you all,' Aunt Sophie scolded as she held her tea towel up like they were all in danger of being flicked. 'Have fun and don't forget to take a phone. And water.'

Poppy nodded and turned back to Sarah. 'Meet us in an hour. We'll get Missy all tacked up and ready to go for you.'

Sarah smiled. 'I have no idea what *tacked up* means, but thanks.'

'It just means we'll have her groomed and with her saddle and bridle on, so she's ready for you to ride.' Poppy was already walking backwards as she explained, feeling like a traitor for wanting to run out the door and bail on her friend so she could get down to the stables. Crystal would seriously be wondering why she wasn't getting as many cuddles and treats as usual.

Minutes later Poppy was yanking on her boots at the back door and racing across the driveway down to the stables. She hadn't even bothered to tie her hair up and it flew out behind her as she ran.

'What's the hurry, Pops?' Uncle Mark called from outside his makeshift wildlife centre.

'Crystal!' she called back, not slowing for a second.

The magpies were calling, the sun was shining and a gentle breeze blew against her face. Starlight Stables was the best place in the world.

Poppy rode Crystal at a walk down the crunchy yellow grass that stretched along the driveway, her friends riding behind her. She was leading Missy so she could take her to Sarah, holding her reins in one hand and the lead rope in the other. Their ponies didn't wear shoes, as Aunt Sophie preferred to keep them all barefoot, so they were careful not to make them walk on the gravel. Aunt Sophie only had shoes on Jupiter because he was training so much, but she liked the other horses to be kept as natural as possible. The farrier had just arrived to trim the horses' hooves, and Poppy smiled at his apprentice as he passed them with a bucket of tools. He grinned back.

'You know, there aren't many cute boys riding around here,' Milly suddenly said.

'Are you looking for a boyfriend?' Poppy teased. 'Or do you like the new farrier?'

Katie giggled. 'Boys are yuck. Believe me, I have brothers.'

Poppy nodded. She was so not into boys. No way. 'Yep, we're best with just girls, I reckon.'

Milly's cheeks were red, which made Poppy bite the inside of her mouth instead of teasing her again. She hadn't meant to embarrass her.

'I was just thinking about it, that's all. You know, how all the top eventing riders are guys, but nearly all of us at pony club and stuff are girls.'

Poppy could tell Milly was super embarrassed now because she was mumbling, and Milly usually always talked loudly and didn't care who heard what she had to say. She bet Milly did like the guy who'd just walked past.

'It is kind of weird.' Poppy had to agree, because she realised it was true. When she watched Badminton or the Olympics, the teams were all made up of men.

'Doesn't mean we can't do it,' Katie said, her voice low but brimming with confidence. 'Girls can do anything.'

'Of course we can!' agreed Milly as she threw her hands in the air dramatically, dropping the reins. 'I wasn't saying we couldn't.'

'Can we just stop talking about boys?' Katie begged as she rode up beside Poppy and leaned low to wrap her arms around Cody's neck in an adoring hug.

Milly rolled her eyes.

'I'm with you, Katie,' Poppy said. She was happy there were no boys around – she saw enough of them at school and at home. She hoped Milly wasn't about to go all boy crazy on her! Besides, Poppy knew she was just as good as any boy. She had her aunt to look up to, and she was one of the best.

'Over here, guys!' Sarah was jumping up and down by the front of the house, so Poppy nudged Crystal in her direction. Her friend was hopping on one foot, trying to get her boot on, and flapping with her other hand. Poppy tried not to laugh as she watched her; Sarah was making a huge effort to fit in, but the whole farm thing just didn't seem to come naturally to her.

'You think she'll ever come back here again?' Katie asked as they rode side by side across the grass towards Sarah.

'Dunno,' Poppy answered honestly. 'I hope so, but I just don't know.'

'Okay, here goes nothing,' Sarah muttered just loud enough for Poppy to hear as she came towards them. 'My legs are sooo sore from sitting up there yesterday.'

'It'll be your butt killing you today after sitting in the saddle for hours!' Milly said cheerily. 'Unless you don't want to come?'

Poppy groaned. 'Do you *always* have to do that?'

'What?' Milly asked innocently.

'We're trying to make her love riding!' Poppy hissed.

'Oops,' Milly said. 'I'm not used to having to be so well behaved.'

'Oh, that actually sounds like a good idea,' Sarah said. 'Don't I have to come?'

Poppy glared at Milly, then jumped down from Crystal and brought Missy closer. She bent and cupped her hands together and smiled when Sarah bent her knee, pleased her friend hadn't been put off riding again. Yet.

'One, two, three!' she counted, boosting Sarah up in the air so she could scramble into the saddle. Poppy helped her guide her boots into the stirrups, positioning them so she had her weight in the balls of her feet.

'You're really, *really* good at all this, Poppy,' Sarah said quietly. When Poppy looked up her friend was watching her intently. 'I never got it, but this is something you're really amazing at. You probably don't even realise, but you are.'

Poppy smiled. Hearing Sarah say that meant a lot to her.

'Thanks,' she mumbled. She wasn't used to praise like that, but she had to admit it felt good for Sarah to see her doing what she loved. At school she did okay at everything, but riding was what she loved and did best.

'So are we going or are we just going to sit around talking all day?' Milly asked.

Poppy threw her arms up in the air. 'She's going to drive me crazy,' she muttered out aloud. They usually all got on so well, but Milly was seriously getting on her nerves today!

'Oops, I forgot lunch,' Sarah said, breaking Poppy's thoughts. 'I left it under the shade by the door.'

'I'll get it,' Poppy said, happy to stalk off to the house for a moment and get away from the others. Maybe it was because Milly wanted to be off racing around and they were going to have to walk, or maybe she was just being way too sensitive about trying to have fun *and* keep Sarah happy, but this weekend wasn't at all like normal.

'Poppy, don't leave me!'

Ooops! Poppy spun around. She'd left Sarah all alone on horseback without keeping hold! She raced back to pick up the rope but saw Katie had already jumped down and grabbed it. Sarah didn't look happy, but luckily Missy hadn't moved.

Poppy touched Sarah's knee, mouthing 'sorry', before turning again and quickly jogging back to the house. She collected up the lunches Sarah had prepared, taking her own backpack off and putting a sandwich, apple and small bag of chips in. She already had her own drink bottle filled up.

'Here we go,' she said, trotting back to the others. She passed food up to Milly first.

'Sorry for being stupid before,' Milly said. 'I wasn't trying to put her off.'

Poppy leaned into Joe and slung her free arm around him. 'Don't worry. Let's just make today really fun for her. You up for it?'

Milly flashed her trademark grin. 'You bet.'

Poppy walked around the back of Cody, one hand on his bottom so he knew she was there and didn't get a fright, and took the lead rope from Katie once she was around the other side. She passed Katie her lunch, made sure her own backpack was on her shoulders firmly and then mounted, keeping hold of the lead rope the entire time. Once she was seated and had her reins gathered in one hand, she looked at her friends.

'Ready?' she asked.

'Ready,' Milly answered first.

'Yep, me too,' Katie said.

Poppy waited, watched Sarah's face for her reaction.

'Let's go before I change my mind,' Sarah said.

Poppy didn't need to be told twice! She pressed her heels to Crystal's side and headed her away from the house, towards the endless parched grass that would lead them across the farm and out to the back paddocks where the cattle would be grazing. She had wire-cutters in her backpack in case they had any fencing problems, plus her mobile so she could take a few pics of them to show her uncle when they returned. She'd done this sort of thing plenty of times with her aunt and uncle, just never on her own.

'I'm hungry already,' Milly said as they rode, all spread out four-abreast as they headed north.

'You're always hungry,' Katie said with a laugh.

'Yeah, but today I'm *super* hungry.'

Joe nickered and made them all laugh. 'I think your pony's ready for lunch too,' Sarah suggested.

'Hey, did you get to help Mark this morning?' Katie asked Sarah. 'I'm absolutely dying to bottle feed one of the babies again.'

'Yeah, it was so cool.' Poppy liked the way Sarah's whole face lit up, like it was the best thing she'd ever done. 'He let me try one of the sling things on, and I fed both kangaroos.'

'It's really sad that he can't keep them. What if they die after they're released?'

Poppy agreed with Katie. 'Uncle Mark always tells me it's for the best, that it's illegal to keep them as pets, but I don't really get it.'

'What!?' Milly exclaimed. 'My parents *ate* kangaroo one night at a restaurant. How can it be legal to eat it and illegal to have one as a pet?'

Poppy shook her head. 'I have no idea.'

They rode in silence for a bit longer. The idea of eating kangaroo grossed Poppy out, same as the idea of eating horse. *Yuck.* She glanced at Sarah and smiled. She was gazing around at the countryside, looking like she'd forgotten all about the fact that she was on the back of a horse.

CHAPTER SEVEN

Adventure Time

They'd been riding for well over an hour, and while she was usually super alert, Poppy wasn't used to just walking like they were in a boring old trek. She hated to think how her friends were feeling – they usually cantered everywhere and found all sorts of things to jump. They were probably bored out of their brains.

As they rode over the farmland, she fell back to daydreaming about the upcoming eventing season, imagining what it would be like to compete every single weekend.

'I think I see them!' Sarah announced, frightening the life out of Poppy. She sat bolt upright in the saddle, eyes peeled. And then she saw them. The black heifers were grazing, their coats gleaming in the sunshine. A few of them stared at the girls as they rode toward them.

'They all look fine,' Poppy said, thankful that she wasn't going to have to deal with any obvious injuries. Her worst fear had been one of them being stuck in a wire fence! But she'd done this often with her aunt and uncle, and she knew that it was usually as easy as looking over each animal to make sure they appeared okay, and checking their grazing and water supplies. 'We'll just need to ride a bit closer to get a good look at them and check their water.'

'Do we all ride over?' Milly asked.

'Hmmm ...' Poppy hadn't really thought the whole thing through. 'I reckon we should all just keep walking, not make a big deal out if it. They might be more likely to let us get close that way, but they should be pretty calm, I reckon.'

'Those bulls look kind of mad,' Katie said as they rode closer. 'Are they acting weird?'

'They're actually heifers, not bulls,' Poppy said, staring at the cattle from where they were halted half a paddock away. 'That means they shouldn't do anything too mad because they don't have any calves at foot.' She kept watching them, and Katie was right. They were acting weirdly, making a lot of noise and milling about anxiously instead of just grazing quietly. It was like they'd been spooked by something. 'The heifer ones are the mums, and they're usually very quiet unless they have babies to protect.'

But the words were hardly out of her mouth when Sarah screamed, 'Poppy!'

One of the cows was snorting and stamping, and all of a sudden it came charging at them!

Poppy felt helpless. She couldn't let go of Sarah's lead rope, but she could feel Missy pulling at it desperately, and Crystal was dancing under her like she wanted to flee. Out of the corner of her eye she saw Sarah lean forward and clutch Missy tightly around the neck in an effort to stay on. Her face was white as a ghost.

The heifer came lunging toward them and Poppy's mind went blank. She moved as close to Sarah as she could and held tight to the lead rope.

Suddenly there was a flash of noise and movement and Milly and Joe plunged in front of her. Milly looked terrified but her legs were clamped down hard on Joe as she yelled and flapped her hands as if she'd gone mad.

Realising what she was doing, Katie leapt forward to join her and the two of them wheeled and turned in fierce circles. Dust flew and their loud yells filled the air.

The cow hesitated, kicking out her legs and snorting, then she turned and trotted off, back to the herd. It was over as suddenly as it had begun.

Poppy could hardly breathe – and she wasn't the one who'd had to ride flatstick at the beast and scare it!

Milly and Katie cantered back and pulled up beside them.

'You guys were . . .' Poppy was lost for words.

'Amazing!' Sarah finished for her. 'Milly, you were so brave, and Katie, I can't believe you just leapt in like that to scare them away.'

Milly and Katie shared shaky smiles but didn't saying anything, probably as much in shock as Poppy was.

'That was incredible,' Poppy finally said. 'You saved us.'

They all sat there, silently, until Sarah spoke up. 'Um. Anyone else think we should ride in the *other direction* before we stop for lunch?' she asked in a quiet voice.

Poppy tried to smile reassuringly, thankful that Sarah had taken charge. 'Yep, how about we go a bit further on along here, towards that boundary paddock. There's a creek with a waterhole a bit further down. Let's check there's water in there still and we can stop under the trees for a bit. I think we could do with a rest.'

The hot summer sun was beating down on them and Poppy's T-shirt was starting to stick to her skin. Her arms were hot, but she always wore sunscreen so she didn't have to worry about burning. It was better than sweating in a long-sleeved shirt.

She gave Crystal a quick pat, keeping an eye on the herd of cattle. The rogue heifer was still assessing them like she could charge again at any minute.

'I'm with you, let's go,' Katie said, walking Cody away from the herd.

They all followed, and Poppy was sure she only started to breathe again after they'd been riding for a few minutes. Up ahead the land fell away into a dip, and Poppy knew that the creek would be at the bottom. Soon enough a large oak tree came into sight, with a wide piece of dried-out dirt stretching across one side.

'*That's* the waterhole?' Milly asked. 'I thought we were going to be able to swim in it!'

Poppy laughed, relieved that someone had broken the silence that had again fallen over them. The waterhole was fed by a creek that sometimes disappeared completely in the middle of summer. Since it was still hot, it was almost all dried up. 'This time of year it's never very impressive, but the horses can have a drink and we can sit in the shade of the tree.'

Poppy glanced over her shoulder at least five times as they rode towards it, worried the stupid cattle might all decide to come after them. She wasn't scared of any animals usually, but she had expected the heifer to be calm and content, so it had made her tummy go all squirmy. Her uncle had always warned her that cattle were unpredictable, that they could kick out back and sideways and every other way in-between, but she hadn't really taken him that seriously until now.

Still, she couldn't shake the feeling that something wasn't quite right. Why had they been making so much noise? What could have spooked them like that and made them so unsettled?

The horses had their ears pricked forward, happy to be out riding across the farm, and Poppy smiled as she looked down at Crystal, her grey ears flicking back every now and again listening for her. Poppy realised she hadn't been talking to her like normal. With Sarah beside her and so much going on, she'd just been sitting in the saddle, forgetting all about her pony except for the odd pat.

'Sorry, girl,' Poppy said. 'I still love you.'

'What?' Sarah asked.

Poppy shrugged. 'Just talking to Crystal.' She found it cute that Missy was walking so close to Crystal – they were almost matching, although Crystal was a little bigger and not as pure white in colour as Missy.

'How do you figure out what to say to her?' Sarah asked. 'I mean, she *is* a horse.'

Poppy rolled her eyes. 'Stop making fun of me. Everyone who loves their horse does it.'

Sarah laughed. 'I'm actually not making fun of you. I want to know.'

'Really?' Poppy wasn't convinced, but still. She loved talking to Crystal. It was natural to her. Whenever she was nervous or doing something new, she talked to her, sometimes even sang a silly song to forget about her nerves. Or she just chatted because it was nice to tell her about what was going on at school and what she wanted to do with her.

'I just tell her stuff. Anything. Just, I don't know.'

'So you don't have to like, force it? I mean you can just talk like we're talking now.'

'Well, she doesn't answer back. She's no talking horse.'

Sarah giggled. 'You're the one being silly now.'

'Hey, Mils, what do you talk to Joe about?' Poppy called ahead. The other two had taken the lead while she was riding at a slower walk with Sarah.

'Whaddya mean? I just talk about nothing. Everything.'

'See?' Poppy shrugged again. 'And I saw you talking to Casper today. It's no different than that.'

'All I told him was that he was a good boy and

113

he had a nice furry belly to scratch.'

'Exactly.' Poppy smiled at Sarah. She couldn't believe they were riding side by side. She never thought it would happen. Not ever!

'I'm starved, how about you?'

Poppy nodded. 'Me, too. Thanks for making us all lunch.'

Sarah burst out laughing. 'It was make lunch or go down to the stables and pick up horse poo. Um, wasn't really something I need to be thanked for! I got the good deal.'

Her laughter was contagious, and Poppy found she couldn't help giggling, even though she personally thought that being stuck inside for an hour when she could be doing *anything* around horses was like torture. There was no way she'd give up an hour of being with Crystal for anything in the world.

They dismounted under the shade of the oak tree, a soft breeze blowing against Poppy's arms, cooling her down. She wished there was more water so they could swim or even just paddle up to their knees, but it didn't look that appealing and it wasn't very deep. There was enough for the horses to drink though, and that was all that really mattered.

She loosened Crystal's girth to let her pony relax while they ate lunch, then ducked under her pony's neck to help Sarah down from Missy. She didn't let go of her until she landed with a soft thud on the ground, followed by a moan.

'How do you ever get used to your body hurting this bad after riding?' Sarah asked.

Poppy thought for a minute. She was often exhausted but never really sore, although she did remember when she'd first started it had made her ache all over, and she always felt it in her leg muscles if she had a break from riding for more than a few weeks.

'I guess you get used to it,' she replied.

Sarah didn't look convinced as she slipped her backpack off her shoulders and held her hand out. 'I'll take yours over for you.'

Poppy gave her backpack to Sarah, undid Missy's girth and told her what a good girl she was, then led both horses side by side to the water's edge, feeling like the filling in a sandwich when they both shied at the same time and squashed her gently between them.

'Easy,' she said in a low voice. 'Nothing to be scared of.'

'Are they a bit jumpy?' Katie asked, appearing beside her.

Poppy frowned. All the ponies seemed to be a little jittery, on high alert, their bodies not as relaxed as they should be when they were about to rest. Each horse knew the routine, that when their girth was slackened off after a ride it meant nothing more was happening for a bit, which made it even more unusual.

'Cody, that's enough!' Milly scolded.

Poppy looked up and saw Cody a bit further down, pawing at the water, his nostrils flared so much that she could see the reddish colour inside them.

'What's going on?' Sarah called out, sitting a few metres away, her back propped up against the trunk of the big oak tree. 'Are they usually like that?'

Poppy stroked Crystal's neck, happy to see that her horse at least was starting to calm down. Or that might have been the Missy effect, because the lovely older pony had dipped her head now and was drinking from the creek. She looked up and saw the other two were still on edge, but whatever it was that had spooked them had passed.

'Do you think they can sense the cattle or something?' Poppy asked Katie in a low voice, not wanting to alarm Sarah. She still hadn't answered her yet and she knew her friend would be asking again what the problem was.

'That was ages back, and they didn't seem worried while we were riding them.'

Something wasn't right, but they had settled enough and Poppy's stomach was roaring with hunger. She waited for Crystal to drink her fill as well, then led them away to a smaller tree beside the oak. She tied Missy properly to a branch with the lead rope, then slipped Crystal's reins more loosely around another. She should have brought a rope for her own pony, but then she hadn't been expecting her to spook over anything.

'Poppy?' Sarah said her name and Poppy turned to find her standing close by, her brows pulled together with worry.

'It's okay. The horses were just worried about something, that's all.'

She watched as Sarah glanced back over her

shoulder, looking for the crazy heifer that had charged them. Horses had amazing senses, knew when something was coming, but something told Poppy it was more than just a cow they were nervous of. They hadn't exactly seemed worried earlier when they were in real danger! In fact, she suspected that Joe and Cody had been super excited about cantering at the cow with Milly and Katie yahooing on their backs.

Maybe there was a change in weather coming?

CHAPTER EIGHT

Trouble

'Come on,' Poppy said, double-checking the horses one last time before linking her arm through Sarah's. 'Let's eat.'

Katie and Milly had tethered their ponies and sat down to join them, and they all unzipped their bags and ate lunch so fast it was like they'd never seen food before.

'Thanks for lunch,' Katie said.

'Yeah, thanks, Sarah,' mumbled Milly, her mouth still full.

'They're just peanut butter and jam sandwiches,' Sarah said with a shrug. 'Nothing special.'

'It's food and it's yummy,' Milly replied. 'Plus

you packed us chips and apples. You're awesome!'

Poppy noticed that Sarah was smiling even though she was staring down at her hands, and Poppy was pleased that they were all having fun together, getting along. She lay back and stared up at the branches waving, just ever so slightly, the pretty green leaves swooshing back and forth and letting little snippets of sunlight peek through. One of the reasons she loved it here was being outside all the time, feeling the sun on her skin and the fresh air against her face. Even when her dad had first died, coming here had been like escaping to a different world. She'd missed her brother and worried about her mum all the time, but it had still been nice to get away and pretend everything was okay. Back then she'd missed Sarah like crazy, which was why having her here was so special.

'What's over there?' Milly asked.

Poppy snapped out of her daydream and propped herself up on her elbows. 'Where?' She stared into the distance, following Milly's point.

'Over there. That black thing.'

Sarah stood, peering forward. Poppy felt too lazy to get up yet so she just watched her.

'It looks like a black pole or something. Weird shape though,' Katie said, yawning as she leaned into Poppy. They were both sitting side by side, and Poppy pushed her head against Katie's and wished she could just close her eyes and sleep for a bit.

'It's a tree,' Sarah declared, taking a few steps away from them. 'But it's black, like it's been charred. Must have been a fire.'

That made Poppy sit bolt upright. She exchanged glances with Katie and they both stood.

'Are you sure? How can you even tell from here?' Poppy asked.

Sarah looked back at Poppy, and Poppy knew from the serious look on her face that she was certain about what she'd seen.

'It's a tree. I've seen them on the news like that. And there's more further out.'

Katie's phone suddenly rang.

'It's Sophie,' Katie said, looking at the screen. They all sat quietly as she answered. 'Hello?'

Katie looked up and locked eyes on Poppy, and Poppy knew straightaway that something was wrong. Seriously wrong.

'She wants to talk to you.'

Poppy reached for the phone. 'Hi, Aunt Sophie.'

'Poppy, you need to come home. There's a storm coming and I need you out of there as quick as you can. Ride safely, but do it fast. Head straight for home, the most direct way you can. I'm already on horseback and I'll meet you somewhere adjacent to Smithy's.'

Poppy's hand started to shake – she couldn't help it. 'How bad is it?' she asked, voice trembling.

'They're expecting lightning, and a fire has already sparked about an hour's drive from here. I want you and your horses back as quick as can be. Do you understand?'

She nodded even though her aunt couldn't see her and quickly stood up. 'We're on our way.'

When she hung up and passed the phone to Katie, she realised her friends were all watching her, silent.

'We need to go,' Poppy announced. 'Pack your bags fast, and get mounted. There's a storm coming.' She stuffing her things into her bag and rushed to the ponies. She tightened Crystal and Missy's girths, checked their bridles and pulled their stirrups back down.

'What kind of storm?' Milly asked, right behind her.

'The kind that sparks a fire. Come on.'

Katie and Sarah didn't say anything, but they were moving fast and Poppy's heart was hammering so loud she was sure they'd be able to hear.

'Is she ready?' Sarah asked.

Poppy turned and gave Sarah a quick smile. 'Ready. We'll be fine, we just need to hurry.'

Sarah looked a lot more confident than she had earlier in the day, or maybe she was just good in emergency situations. 'I'm okay. You were right about her being a sweet pony.' Sarah stroked Missy on the cheek and Poppy thought she was going to burst she was so excited about how friendly Sarah was being with the little horse.

'She *is* super sweet. Before Crystal came along she was my favourite pony here.' Poppy patted Missy and put the reins over her neck. 'Let's get you back in the saddle.'

Poppy gave Sarah a leg up and then mounted herself, settling into the saddle and gathering her reins in one hand, the lead rope in the other. She was used to leading another horse to exercise two at once, so it didn't bother her having Missy beside her, even if they were going to be going faster than planned. Milly and Katie were already mounted and ready to go, and she could see from the look on Milly's face that she was ready to dig her heels into Joe's side and go as fast as they could to get back.

'Why don't you guys stay in front?' Poppy said, knowing that she had to balance the danger with getting back fast. She still had to make sure it was safe for Sarah, and her friends knew their way around the farm. 'We'll go as quick as we can but you two can set your own pace to keep your ponies happy.' She was desperate to gallop with them, but she knew she had to keep Sarah safe.

'You sure?' Katie asked. 'We'll still stay close.'

Poppy nodded, and Milly burst into a canter, taking off and leaving Katie to play catch up. Crystal thrust her head in the air and started to jig-jog, but Poppy sat deep in the saddle and tightened her reins.

'Not today, girl. We're just going steady.' Crystal wasn't impressed, her body like a taut rubber band beneath Poppy, but she started to calm down once the other two horses were further into the distance.

They'd ridden a long, long way from the stables, and Poppy knew heading home was when Crystal always started to get excited.

The other farms surrounding Starlight were home to horses too, which was why they were all allowed to ride over each other's land. They had jumps scattered down most of the fence lines, and Poppy watched as Joe soared over a fence up ahead, followed by Katie on her palomino. Poppy would have to find a gate to lead Sarah through – Milly had definitely chosen the most direct route back.

'Sorry you have to babysit me,' Sarah apologised.

'Don't be crazy.' Poppy felt guilty because she had kind of been wishing that Sarah wasn't there so she could race off. 'The storm will be a way off yet. Sophie was just being cautious.'

'Thanks, though.' Sarah smiled when Poppy looked across at her.

'Hey, I bet you didn't want to be sitting in your room watching DVDs every weekend with me when Dad died,' Poppy said, taking a big breath. She'd practically lived at Sarah's house when they'd first found out that her dad wouldn't be coming home. 'Or listening to me cry all the time. I think you've done plenty of babysitting me too.'

'You're my best friend, Pops.' Sarah looked like she had tears in her eyes and Poppy realised that she did, too. She quickly brushed them away. Sometimes talking about her dad was okay; other times it made her want to cry her eyes out and hide under a doona for the rest of the day, curled up in bed.

They were almost at the fence line now, and Poppy was looking around for somewhere they could get over that didn't involve jumping when the rumble of hooves made her head snap up. What was going on?

'How close did Sophie say that other fire was?' Sarah asked, as if she was reading Poppy's mind.

Just as Poppy was about to answer, she saw Milly and Katie riding back towards them. Milly was waving one hand frantically. They were still a way away, but Poppy's body was suddenly covered in goosebumps. Why were they coming back? Something was definitely up.

Poppy looked up at the sky. The clouds were starting to look strange. There were swirling, murky grey ones swallowing the fluffy white clouds that had been sitting peacefully still in the bright blue sky while they'd been having their lunch. Poppy knew that because she'd been admiring them every time the leaves parted.

'The weather's changing here already,' Poppy shifted in the saddle, gripping her reins a little tighter as Crystal started to dance beneath her. She cast a quick look at Missy, saw that the little pony looked more alert than usual. 'It's okay though, just a little wind.'

She didn't tell Sarah her suspicions – that this was why the horses and cows had been spooked before, and that the only reason Aunt Sophie had phoned them was because she was super worried. Sophie didn't overreact to anything. Not ever.

She got off Crystal when they approached a gate, opening it quickly and getting the two horses through before mounting again. She was just pushing her feet into the stirrup irons when a thundering of hooves made her look up.

'Poppy!' Katie yelled out as she and Milly neared, pulling Cody up hard so he came to an almost dead stop from a canter. Something was *definitely* bad for Katie to be behaving like that. She never yanked on her pony's mouth! His sides were heaving, his nostrils flared from blowing hard.

'What's wrong?' said Poppy.

Then she saw that Katie was holding her mobile.

'It was Mrs D,' Katie panted, still breathless. 'She said there's another fire and it's much closer this time.'

The wind came through with a whooshing noise then and Poppy cringed, goosebumps again rippling across her arms. They definitely didn't want to get caught out in this storm, and if there was another fire . . .

She gulped. They needed to move.

She checked her watch, saw that they'd been gone about three hours including their lunch break. It wouldn't have taken them half that time usually because they'd be cantering and racing each other, but it was slow going at a walk, which meant they needed to go faster.

Poppy looked up, overwhelmed. It was too much to deal with. The weather, figuring out which way to go, how to make sure Sarah was safe when they didn't have time to walk, and now another fire.

'Poppy?' Katie cried, her voice almost a scream.

A big plop of rain landed on Poppy's arm. She tipped her head back and looked up at the sky, ignoring the fact that Crystal was starting to shift nervously beneath her. She needed time to think. Poppy shut her eyes, wondering if the fact that rain was coming would make it less likely for a fire to start, but she knew how dry the grass was, that it would have to bucket down with rain to put out any fires or stop one from spreading. She couldn't even figure out the safest way to get home – away from trees – that would still get them back quickly.

'Poppy.' This time it was Sarah saying her name. Her friend's voice was quiet, calm. And just what she needed to hear.

Poppy opened her eyes, sat up straight and a plan formed in her mind. She could do this. Her friends were depending on her and so was Aunt Sophie. Milly had arrived now, and both she and Katie were watching her intently.

'We need to get back fast before the worst of it hits, and I think I know where we're best to ride,' explained Poppy. 'But I need you guys to stay close this time.'

'Oh, but we rode for hours to get here!' Milly

moaned. 'Should we all jump back over the fence?'

'No,' Poppy said. 'No jumping. And we need to stay this side anyway. I'm going to get Sarah up behind me. She can hold on to me tight, and that means we can canter back. It'll be safer and way faster.'

'No way,' Sarah protested, looking terrified. Her eyes were wide. 'I can't do it.'

'Yes, you can,' Poppy replied. 'You've been riding like a pro, so I know you can do it.' She nodded at the others. 'I want you two to keep the horses calm, then Katie, you can help Sarah up while Milly holds Cody.'

She filled her lungs with air, another big plop of rain cold against her skin.

'We're going home a different way to get back faster. Down the side here, following this property, then back down by the bush. It's much shorter.'

'Poppy, we can't ride through trees in a bad storm. That's crazy,' Katie said.

'No, but we can ride alongside the trees. It'll be way faster than the way we came.' So long as they stayed a safe distance away, they'd be fine. She hoped.

Her friends still looked like they were in shock, but Poppy was feeling confident now. Aunt Sophie trusted her and Poppy knew the farm like the back of her hand. The worst that could happen was the horses would spook or that lightning would strike too close, but she just had to do her best.

'Come on. We need to get going,' she ordered.

Katie turned Cody around and Milly nodded.

'You're sure about this?' Sarah asked, her voice barely a mumble.

'Yep,' Poppy replied. She was still nervous, but she'd come up with a plan, and she was going to stick to it.

CHAPTER NINE

Lightning Strikes

Sarah was clinging on to Poppy so hard that Poppy was struggling to breathe. She shortened her reins, tightened her grip on Missy's lead rope and braced herself for the worst.

'You okay?' she asked Sarah.

Her friend just squeezed her tighter around the middle. Poppy doubted she'd ever fall off she was holding so tight! The horses were super jittery now, and Crystal felt tightly coiled beneath her, body quivering she was so desperate to flee.

'Let's go!' she shouted, her voice whisked away on the roaring wind and almost impossible to hear. 'I'll set the pace!'

Poppy was leading and she asked Crystal to walk before pushing her straight into a canter. It would be too hard for Sarah to balance to a bumpy trot, but Poppy had to fight Crystal to keep their canter steady when her pony wanted to flatten out and gallop for home. It would have been easier to get Katie to lead Missy, but Poppy knew neither she or Milly had any experience riding and leading at the same time, and she wanted to make sure she got everyone back safely.

The wind whipped against her face and a rumble of thunder nearly made her jump, but Poppy focused on where she was heading. She knew that if she stayed calm and didn't panic, that Crystal would feel it and keep her head. If she was a ball of nerves, then her horse would sense it and freak out, which would be super dangerous for her and Sarah.

'Sarah!' she yelled out, hoping Sarah would hear her. 'Hold on to me tight around the tummy.' Poppy couldn't help her friend other than tell her what to do. She was holding her reins with one hand and Missy's lead rope with the other.

'I'm scared!' Sarah screamed back.

'You'll be okay!' Poppy gritted her teeth. Sarah

might be scared, but so long as she held on she'd be fine. And a whole lot safer than riding on her own.

Crystal shied when a blast of wind sent a branch cracking down from a tree nearby, but Poppy stayed firmly seated in the saddle. Just like glue, she muttered to herself. That's what Aunt Sophie had always said to her, and she was pleased that she'd had to ride without reins and stirrups so often. It had stopped her from relying on anything other than her own legs and bottom for balance.

She quickly looked back and saw that Katie and Milly were both fine, although she bet Joe was fighting for his head, used to being in front. He loved being the leader and he didn't like it unless he had at least his nose in front of the other ponies.

They kept cantering together, Missy going fast to keep up with Crystal, and as the ground flew beneath them the horses began to settle. The poor things would be exhausted by the time they got back, thought Poppy. The air felt cold now but Poppy was hot from riding, her face felt flushed and her lungs burned from breathing so hard. She wanted to check her watch to see how long they'd been going – it seemed like they had been riding for ages – but staying in control of both horses was challenging enough. The whole ride had passed by in a blur.

They were nearing the trees when a bolt of lightning suddenly lit up the sky, the blast of brightness finished off with a loud boom of thunder. Crystal shied at the same time as Missy pulled hard on the rope, rearing beside them. Oh man. They were in big trouble now. Poppy had no idea if Aunt Sophie would already be close or if she'd been ringing and they hadn't heard. She pulled back to slow Crystal down, refusing to let go of the little grey when they were finally close to home. She couldn't bear it if she lost Missy now.

Katie suddenly appeared on Cody, riding close to Missy and boxing her in so she couldn't dart sideways. She could still bolt forward, but having the other horses beside her seemed to help calm her down.

'Thanks!' Poppy yelled out. She didn't know if Katie had heard her or not because another bolt of lightning scared the life out of her, the thunder going on and on.

If the thunder comes straight after with no delay,

it means the lightning is close. She remembered Uncle Mark telling her that and it was something that had stuck in her brain. A shiver ran down her spine and she pushed Crystal back into a fast canter, knowing her friends would be able to keep up no matter how fast she was going.

The sky was swirling now but Poppy did her best to ignore it. More lightning made Crystal throw her head up and rear, her scared whinny sounding more like a scream.

'Poppy!' Sarah yelled in her ear, and held Poppy so tight she could hardly breathe, tipping to the side and almost dragging them both off sideways.

Poppy struggled to stay in the saddle as Sarah yanked herself back up. 'Keep holding on! We're nearly there!' she cried. Poppy knew it was safer to slow down now rather than spook the horses more, even if did mean being stuck out in the storm for longer. They couldn't risk falling off or the horses getting away on them.

She slowed Crystal down, talking to her in a soothing voice, trying to make her feel safe. 'Whoa, girl, we're fine. It's just some silly wild weather.'

They rode alongside the edge of the forest,

careful to stay away from the trees in case any large branches fell. The lurching, creaking sounds of the blue gums were scaring the horses, but Poppy knew this was the quickest way, and it was the only way back that meant they didn't have to dismount and open gates or jump fences. There was no way she could do that with Sarah riding double.

'Poppy!' Milly screamed. 'Fire!'

Poppy spun around in her saddle fast, forgetting Sarah was holding onto her, and had to grab for Crystal's mane to stop from falling off. Sarah turned too, and gasped. Poppy felt her arms tighten around her stomach again so hard that she thought she was going to be sick. Behind them, a tree had been struck by the lightning and she could see the beginning of flames and black smoke curling into the air. The red burst of fire was terrifying as it spread across the trunk.

We're in big trouble now.

The next crack of lightning was deafening, and it was followed swiftly by a ferocious rumble of thunder. It was all so close. Too close. Poppy bit the inside of her mouth to stop from crying out. What were they supposed to do?

'We need to get out of here,' she yelled, fighting to be heard over the roar of the weather. The rain hadn't come to much yet, but she knew that when it started it would absolutely pour down. Would this be enough to stop the fire? Even though riding through a storm wasn't ideal, it was better than fire. Please let it rain soon, she prayed.

'Let's go!' Katie yelled back, her eyes wide. Even Cody, who was usually the calmest of the ponies, was jumping around, his body quivering, the whites of his eyes making him look like a wild horse.

Poppy knew they had to move, but her eyes were glued to the tree. Flames were already licking up the tree, swallowing it, rapidly engulfing the leaves and branches. It was close enough to the bush and other trees that Poppy knew it would spread fast once the branches started to crack and fall to the ground. The grass around was so dry and then . . . She gulped, biting back tears. Would it race all the way to Starlight Stables?

Ohmigod. Where was Aunt Sophie?

'We need to call Sophie. Now!' she cried, riding closer to Katie so they were in a huddle. Milly joined them, one hand on Joe's neck as she muttered soothing words to him. 'She needs to know how close the fire is to Starlight!'

'What about the koala we saw the other day? And her baby! That was near here,' Sarah said desperately, her mouth close to Poppy's ear. 'Will they die?'

Poppy shuddered. Sarah was right. And koalas were so slow, that's why so many of them were killed in bushfires. 'There's nothing we can do,' she said, knowing they couldn't risk getting any closer to the fire. They weren't far from home now, but they needed to warn Aunt Sophie.

Katie was yelling into the phone, and when Poppy went to gather up her reins tighter, ready to get going again, Sarah's scream made her jump.

'It's the koala!' Sarah yelled. 'She's right there!'

Poppy's heart leapt when she realised what Sarah was pointing at. Near the edge of the bush, running and stumbling, was a koala.

'We can't just leave her,' Milly said, a defiant look on her face that Poppy knew spelled trouble.

'Please, Poppy. We have to!' Sarah begged.

'No, we can't,' Poppy said, looking up at the sky, listening to another rumble and then glancing over her shoulder to make sure the fire hadn't spread.

To her horror she saw that the fire had raced across a small piece of grass to another tree. It was well behind them but too close for comfort. She knew how fast a bushfire could move. Faster than a car . . . much faster than a horse galloping. Her stomach was flip-flopping again. She didn't want the koala to get hurt, but . . .

'There could be other animals in there,' Milly said.

'We can't help them. There's nothing we can do,' Poppy said firmly. She didn't want to leave the koala to die in the flames. But it was also up to her to get them to safety.

Katie hung up the phone. 'Sophie is coming. I told her where we are, and she said the fire brigade is on their way as well as a helicopter with monsoon buckets.'

More thunder cracked and Joe reared and let out a shrill whinny. Poppy almost lost her grip on Missy again when she tried to pull away.

'Whoa!' Poppy said, both hands on the reins now as she tried to steady Crystal. The mare was stamping her feet and Poppy knew they only had minutes to react before the fire spread like crazy. The horses were spooking worse than ever and she needed to come up with a plan.

'I'm not leaving without that koala,' Milly yelled, and Poppy knew she was being serious. When Milly decided something, she never backed down.

'Katie, hold Missy,' Poppy said, digging her heels into Crystal's side to move closer to Cody. She passed the rope over, waited till she could see that Katie had a firm grip. Katie looked at her, eyes wide and frightened. But she nodded gamely. 'If she gets away she should run home, but try to keep hold.'

'Let's go get that koala!' Poppy said to Milly, determined. She was only going for it because it was so near to them, and the fire was still a way off behind them, but they had to act fast. She pressed her legs to Crystal and they rocketed towards the koala. She was worried her pony would resist riding towards the fire, but she did exactly what was asked of her. And within seconds Poppy was pulling Crystal up, stopping a few metres from the koala.

Sarah suddenly let go of her.

'What are you doing?' Poppy yelled.

But Sarah either didn't hear or didn't care,

slithering to the ground before Poppy could stop her. Poppy jumped off too, thrusting her reins to Milly and hoping she'd be able to hold Crystal. If her pony bolted, they'd be in terrible danger. Thunder boomed again and Poppy braced for more lightning, hoping it didn't strike another tree.

'Help me!' Sarah was already standing by the koala, but it was no longer moving. Poppy watched as Sarah yanked her backpack off, and she quickly realised what her plan was. Poppy ran towards her and helped her empty it, dumping everything on the ground. Her own backpack was strapped to Missy, so she'd been able to double with Sarah behind her, and she was pleased that her friend's was the larger pack and that she'd thought so quickly on her feet.

Poppy kept an eye on the fire in the forest back where they'd just ridden past, a lump in her throat making it hard to swallow. The fire was starting to spread greedily, moving to another tree, the red flames licking fast. The air was warmer now, the heat from the fire spreading, smoke starting to curl into her lungs. She pulled her eyes away, focused on the koala. The fire wasn't so close that she needed to panic . . . yet.

'His paws are burned bad. That's why he's not moving anymore,' Sarah said.

Poppy grabbed Sarah's drink bottle. She knew they didn't have much time but the poor koala was terrified and probably thirsty. She couldn't believe it when the animal touched one of its damaged paws to her hand, the other on the bottle, as Poppy tipped it and let him drink. The koala knew exactly what she was trying to do, that they were trying to help him!

'I can't believe it!' Poppy exclaimed. Sarah grinned back at her.

'Hurry!' Milly screamed from her horse.

Poppy prised the bottle from the koala and grabbed the backpack. While she was opening it, Sarah gathered up the animal, the look of awe on her face something Poppy was sure she'd never forget.

'He's not even trying to hurt me,' Sarah said softly.

Poppy was so proud of her for picking up a wild animal. She might not love horses like Poppy did, but she had been so brave helping with the koala. Sarah placed him carefully in the backpack and

Poppy zipped it up as much as she could without hurting the scared animal.

'I hope he won't fall out.' Sarah looked as worried as Poppy felt.

'He'll be fine. But we need to go!'

There was a loud crack then and Poppy panicked, not wanting to let the fire come any closer to them. She lifted the pack as Sarah held out her arms, and secured it on her friend's back.

'Run!' she yelled. She was faster than Sarah but it meant she had time to grab hold of Crystal when Milly thrust the reins at her. Joe was freaking out big time and she was having a hard time controlling him. Poppy thrust one foot in the stirrup and left the other for Sarah.

'Quick, put your foot in there and I'll pull you up.'

Crystal was almost prancing on the spot and Sarah kept missing her footing.

'I can't!' she cried.

Poppy shook her head, determined. 'You can. Lift up, hold onto me, and I'll help.'

Sarah was heavier to pull than Poppy had realised, but finally she was in the saddle behind her, arms clamped around Poppy's waist.

Joe reared again and bolted, and Poppy bet that Milly had no chance of holding him any longer. Crystal followed and Poppy let her canter fast. Her pony had two girls on her back plus a koala, but she was acting like she was carrying no weight at all she was moving so quick!

The rest of the bush that was untouched by fire rushed past them in a blur as they galloped.

Please let the koala be okay. Please let it not fall out, prayed Poppy. Now they had rescued it, the last thing she wanted was for it to fall and hurt itself even worse.

Suddenly, Aunt Sophie appeared ahead of them. Katie was way up front, looking like she was struggling to keep hold of Missy, and when Sophie neared, Missy pulled free and galloped past her. Poppy's heart sunk, but Missy still had her reins over her neck, which meant she shouldn't get caught up in them.

Poppy had no idea how fast the fire was spreading or what was going to happen, but she was sure they were going to be okay. They weren't that far from home and they could just keep riding if they had to. She wasn't going to let the fire come close to her pony!

A loud whirr jolted her from her thoughts and made her look up. She imagined it was more thunder, part of the storm, and then she saw the big, powerful machine in the sky. It was a helicopter carrying a huge bucket. Just as she was thinking that one bucket wouldn't do much, as the fire roared loud and sent shivers through her all over again, the sky opened up and the rain poured down like a tap had been turned on full. She couldn't imagine what it would be like to see the farm burned, the bush they loved to ride through gone or charred black, so the rain was the most beautiful, amazing thing she'd ever seen. Rain this hard would surely have to put the fire out!

Tears stung her eyes and streamed down as they continued to canter. Today was supposed be a fun day with her friends, an adventure, and instead it had turned out to be a disaster. And what about the mother koala and her baby? Did they have the mother in their backpack and her baby was still out there, burned or terrified? Or was this a different koala?

Poppy clenched her teeth together, refusing to think about the animals that could have been in those trees. They'd done everything they could, and they'd saved an injured animal.

The stables came into view then and Poppy almost sobbed in relief. They were home.

CHAPTER TEN

Koala Crazy

'Are you all okay?' Aunt Sophie's face was flushed as she dismounted and hauled the reins over Jupiter's neck, her eyes searching Poppy's face for a moment before turning to the other girls now they were outside the stables.

Their ponies were heaving, and when Poppy ran a hand down Crystal's neck she realised her pony was soaked with sweat. Poppy touched her own wet cheeks, wanting to brush the tears away, but her hand was shaking so much she just dropped it back onto Crystal's neck. The horses all seemed calmer now they were back, or maybe they were just too exhausted from being ridden so hard to do anything other than stand. They'd cantered all the way in from the fire and hadn't been cooled down, and Poppy had no idea what they were supposed to do next.

The rain continued to fall and Poppy realised her T-shirt was soaking. Aunt Sophie rushed over and helped Sarah down, then Poppy dismounted, her legs wobbling when her feet hit the ground.

'Take the koala into the wildlife hospital,' Poppy told Sarah.

'Koala?' Aunt Sophie asked.

Poppy pointed at the black nose and soft ears poking out of Sarah's backpack. Aunty Sophie's eyes widened. She didn't say anything, just grabbed her phone and dialled. Poppy knew without being told that the heavy rain would probably stop the fire from spreading, that they'd been so lucky, but she also knew it was better to be safe.

'Follow me,' Poppy called out, taking Jupiter's reins and leading both him and Crystal into the stables. 'Tie them all up, take their gear off and we'll get them to the safe paddock.'

She heard the clip-clop of hooves over concrete and knew that her friends were following her. They hastily tied up together and removed saddles and bridles, and even though Poppy felt terrible that the horses were heaving so much, she knew they had to act fast.

'It's Missy!' Milly's shout made Poppy stop what she was doing and dart under Jupiter's neck and out the door.

'I'll get her,' Poppy said, holding out a hand and smiling at the pretty grey as she trotted, head held high, towards her. Her heart leapt at seeing the pony uninjured. The lead rope was dangling and Poppy managed to grab it as she came closer. It helped that the other horses were all there, otherwise she doubted it would have been so easy.

Poppy quickly led Missy in and took her saddle off too, and passed the rope to Milly.

'Come on,' she said, when they'd all finished.

Katie was the first to follow as she only had one pony to lead, although Poppy couldn't actually see her over Jupiter. It was lucky the big horse was so well behaved, because she was way too short to deal with a giant like him if he was naughty!

'Do you think the koala is okay? Did he scratch you?' Katie asked.

Poppy smiled, thinking of how cute the furry animal had been. 'He was so cute. He even drank from the drink bottle when I held it!'

'I can't believe how close we were to that fire,' Milly said, not far behind them. 'That was so scary.'

Poppy didn't even want to think about the fire and what it could have done to the land she loved so much, to all the animals that could have been injured or killed. The rain drenched them as they walked, but the thunder had stopped and Poppy hoped the lightning had, too. She'd never been scared of a storm before, but then again she'd never seen lightning strike a tree down either!

'It wasn't the baby with its mum, was it?' Katie asked, her voice full of sadness.

'No,' Poppy admitted. 'Or if it was, there was no sign of the baby.'

They led the horses in silence the rest of the way, letting them go only once they were all inside the safe paddock. The other horses were already in there. Aunt Sophie must have moved them as soon as they told her about the fire, or maybe the minute she heard about the storm. Poppy watched as Jupiter trotted away, Crystal sticking by his side and cantering to keep up with him. Cody, Joe and Missy walked more slowly to join their friends. They were obviously exhausted.

Poppy couldn't imagine what it would be like to see fire spread rapidly across the farm, taking over every blade of grass, every tree . . . She squeezed her hands into fists. *The stables.*

'The fire's out!' Aunt Sophie called, standing at the gate and waving, mobile pressed to her ear. 'The monsoon buckets had nothing on that rain. The weather started the fire, but it saved us, too.'

Poppy grabbed hold of Katie's hand. Milly grabbed her other hand and they all stood for a moment in the rain, looking at each other in relief.

'Come on, girls!' Aunt Sophie called. 'I hear you've got a koala to show me!'

Poppy forgot all about the terror of the fire and burst out laughing. Her hair was plastered to her face, dripping down her neck and into her eyes. Even her boots felt like they were full of water!

She grinned at her friends. Everything was going to be okay.

'You girls sure know how to find trouble, huh?'
Uncle Mark said, not looking up from his assessment
of the koala.

'This one wasn't my fault,' Milly said, hands on
her hips, dripping. 'It was all of us.'

Poppy smiled over at Milly. 'We couldn't just
ride away.'

They huddled around, shoulders pressed tightly
together, and gazed down at the injured animal.

'Can we call him Bill? You know, after Blinky
Bill?' Sarah asked.

Mark laughed. 'You could,' he said, looking up
from bandaging the little guy's last paw, 'but I don't
know if that's a very good name for a girl.'

Poppy giggled. 'Maybe Blinky Belinda then.'

Her friends were all laughing too, but then
Sarah spoke up. 'Mark, we saw a koala and her baby
yesterday. Do you think this could be the mum?'

He frowned. 'I doubt it. A mother would still be
producing milk for a joey, even if it was big enough
to be riding on her back, and I doubt this girl is
more than two years old. She's not old enough to
have a joey that size yet.'

The koala was sitting there, looking up at them

with her big brown eyes like it was the most normal thing in the world for four humans to be standing around her. She was so beautiful and Poppy was so proud that they'd saved her.

'It was Sarah who thought to put her in the backpack,' Poppy blurted out, wanting everyone to know that Sarah was the one to be praised, not her. 'She just scooped her up and put her in.'

'That was very brave of you, Sarah,' Aunt Sophie said from the other side of the shed. She was tending to the other babies while they watched Mark.

'Her paws are badly burned, but she's got a great chance of healing up just fine,' Mark said. 'You girls did a great thing saving her today. I'm really proud of you all for thinking so quickly in an emergency.'

Poppy wasn't so sure Aunt Sophie would like the fact that they'd spent a few minutes saving a koala when the fire was spreading behind them!

'What now?' Milly asked.

'Well,' Uncle Mark said, taking off his surgical gloves and throwing them in a bin. 'I'm going to put Blinky Belinda somewhere safe and then we're all heading up to the house for dinner.'

Poppy yawned. She hadn't realised how tired she was. Her stomach rumbled. Or how hungry!

'I'll go down and take the horses some hay. They can stay there all night. It won't do them any harm,' Aunt Sophie said. 'There are pizzas in the freezer. Can you girls get them out and pop them in the oven for me?'

Poppy nodded. 'Sure thing.'

Katie and Milly both turned to follow her, but Sarah stayed still.

'I'm going to wait for Belinda to settle in, talk to her for a little bit. If that's okay with you, Mark?' Sarah asked.

Poppy's uncle smiled and gave Sarah a pat on the shoulder. 'You saved her, you can do the honours,' he said. 'How about I show you how to pick her up properly and you can bring her over.'

Poppy happily left Sarah to it. She deserved to be the one helping after what she'd done.

'You were right about her being awesome,' Katie said as they walked out of the makeshift hospital and headed for the house. It was only raining lightly now, but Poppy's boots were still making a squelching sound and she shivered in her wet T-shirt.

'Yeah, she is,' she smiled.

'I feel bad for saying that I didn't know why you were friends with her,' Milly confessed. 'That was so stupid. She's fun and super brave, and I can't believe she actually rode all the way back! That was pretty awesome to gallop like that on her second ride.'

Poppy slung an arm around Milly, pulling her in tight. Milly laughed and they all linked arms and ran the rest of the way to the house.

'I hope those other koalas are safe,' Katie said.

'Yeah, me too.' Poppy let go of her friends and leaned against the side of the house to take her boots off. She tipped them up to get some water out, then took off her dripping wet socks and squeezed them out. She looked down and realised that it was probably a good idea to take her jods off too. She didn't want to drip water through the house. 'I'm going to strip off here.'

Two minutes later they were running through the house in their undies and T-shirts, racing each other for the bathroom. Poppy leapt up the stairs, but Milly got to the bathroom first and raced in, claiming the shower.

'Ugh,' Poppy moaned, slumping down outside

the bathroom and sinking onto the carpet. She was desperate for a hot shower.

'I'm already dreaming of my warm hoodie, thick socks and a hot Milo,' Katie said.

'Oooooh, me too!' Poppy sighed, exhausted. 'Oh, I forgot about the pizza.'

'Make Milly do it when she's out,' Katie said.

Poppy laughed. It had been a crazy day, and for once they couldn't even blame Milly for it.

Meow.

Poppy sat up straight, blinking, wondering if she'd just imagined it.

'Did you hear that?' Katie asked.

Poppy laughed. 'Was that you being stupid?'

Meow.

Poppy stood up, peered down the hall, certain Sarah was about to jump out from somewhere. And then she saw a little blur of black disappearing into their bedroom. She padded down the hall, toes sinking into the thick carpet. She peered into the room and then clamped her hand over her mouth. 'It's the wild cat! It's Ghost!'

Katie put her hands on Poppy's shoulders as she looked into the room. 'Looks like you and Sarah are sharing the bed with someone else tonight.'

The little black kitten yawned as it watched them, before kneading in a circle and then curling into a ball on Poppy's pillow.

'At least she's not cold and alone.'

Katie laughed. 'Yeah. If you don't mind wet cat on your pillow!'

Poppy was about to answer when she heard the bathroom door open. She raced past Katie and scooted down the hall, almost knocking Milly over as she leapt into the bathroom.

Yes! She stripped off the rest of her clothes, turned the hot water on and jumped into the shower. So she had to share her bed with a wet cat. She didn't care. All she cared about was being at Starlight Stables, with her friends sharing her room and her pony safe in a paddock she could see from the window. In fact, she grinned as the hot water poured down, the more animals the better.

CHAPTER ELEVEN

Home Time

The rest of the weekend went by in a blur, and Poppy could hardly believe that it was only yesterday that they'd ridden for their lives across the farm, racing for safety as the fire breathed down their necks like a dragon chasing them down. Now all the ponies were grazing quietly in their paddocks as if nothing had happened.

'I can't believe we didn't ride today,' Milly moaned.

'Seriously?' Katie said, rolling her eyes at Milly. 'After yesterday I think your poor pony deserved a day off.'

Poppy hated missing a day riding too, but they'd

had fun feeding the baby animals and watching the koala. Sarah had hardly left Belinda's side except to come out for lunch, and now it was almost time to go. Because the fire hadn't spread, it was almost like the whole thing had never happened.

A toot signalled that Katie's mum had arrived, and Poppy looked at her friends. It was only another two weeks before they were back, but it always felt like a lifetime to wait. She still hated saying goodbye.

'See you soon,' Poppy said, giving Katie a quick hug, then Milly.

'Promise you'll come back?' Katie asked Sarah as she threw her arms around her.

'If the koala is still here, I will!'

They all laughed at Sarah, but Poppy knew she wasn't joking. Sarah just didn't like horses the way she did, and that was okay. They'd still had fun together, and if Sarah wanted to come back again then Poppy wouldn't feel bad leaving her to go riding if it meant her friend could enjoy helping Uncle Mark with the farm animals. It was just nice having her at Starlight, no matter what they were doing.

Casper let out a loud woof and made them all jump.

'Casper!' Milly scolded, dropping and throwing her arms around him. He rolled over, and Milly kissed him before rising and waving.

Poppy watched them drive away, standing beside Sarah in the late sunshine.

'We need to grab our bags,' she finally sighed. 'My mum will be here any minute.'

Sarah looked back over her shoulder and Poppy knew exactly what she was thinking.

'You want to go back in one last time, don't you?' Poppy asked.

Sarah nodded. Poppy had to admit that she loved the koala too. It was impossible to think that an animal so sweet was actually wild, especially after she'd trusted them enough to let them help her and get her to safety.

'I'll get your stuff and mine,' Poppy said.

Sarah grinned and Poppy threw her arms around her. It might not have been the weekend she'd had planned, but it had been pretty awesome.

'I know you're not going to believe it, but I kind of loved it here,' Sarah said in her ear.

Poppy stepped back and laughed. 'Seriously?'

'I don't think I'll ever love horses like you do, but I get it. The animals, your awesome aunt and uncle, it's pretty cool.' She giggled. 'And Mark asked me to come back to help out whenever I wanted. I think I might like to be a vet one day.'

'That's so cool.' Poppy hugged her tight again. 'It was a pretty amazing weekend, fire or no fire. I'm so pleased you like it here.'

'Come on, Casper,' Sarah called out.

The big dog wagged his tail and got up, trotting beside Sarah all the way back to the shed. Poppy couldn't wipe the smile off her face as she watched her friend. Now she knew for sure that she'd get Sarah back to Starlight again one day.

'It's been two weeks,' Milly said. 'There's no way we're going to find them.'

Poppy rolled her eyes at Milly. Sometimes she was just so impatient! 'Koalas don't move a lot. That's why it never works when people try to relocate them. They always end up coming back to their home.'

Katie was trailing behind, scanning the trees as well. 'I can't believe that Belinda's paws are looking so good. Pity Sarah couldn't come this weekend.'

Poppy felt bad about not bringing Sarah. For the first time it had been Sarah begging to come, but her parents hadn't let her because they had some family dinner to go to. She'd promised Sarah that the minute she arrived she'd go out searching for the mother and baby they'd seen together.

'She's here!' Milly shrieked.

'You mean she *was*,' Katie called out, 'before you frightened the life out of her!'

Poppy pushed Crystal into a trot and quickly joined Milly at the same time as Katie pulled up beside her.

'It's her,' Poppy said. 'It has to be.'

They all stood there, gazing up at the koala with the big joey on her back. She was chewing a leaf, blinking down at them, baby peering over her ears.

'I knew she'd be okay,' Katie whispered. 'I just knew it.'

Belinda was on the mend, the koala and her baby were safe, the horses were all okay and she was back in the saddle again. They'd been out to check on the cattle, too. The part of bush they were riding through was untouched by the fire, but Poppy shuddered when she thought about the burned, blackened trees where the fire had ignited. This koala was lucky, but she knew that so many more koalas had probably been injured by bushfire elsewhere over the weekend. They were doubly lucky that the Delaney's neighbour had a helicopter and a monsoon bucket ready in case of fire, not to mention the torrential rainfall.

'Let's leave her in peace,' Poppy said. 'We don't want to scare her.'

'Last one to the log is a rotten rat!' Milly declared, taking off and leaving them for dead.

'Milly!' Poppy yelled. She raced after her, Katie close on her heels.

'I win!' Milly shouted as she flew over the log.

Poppy and Katie ended up midair at the same time, jumping side by side and landing with a thump together. Milly was still cantering ahead of them and Poppy kept her heels down, bottom out of the saddle, as they raced after her friend.

'Come on, Crystal!' she urged as her pony stretched out beneath her. They shot past Milly when the track widened again.

'Woo hoo!' she cried, punching the air.

'I'll get you for that!' Milly yelled.

Poppy just laughed. 'You can try!' She kept her legs tight against Crystal and urged her forward, sun on her skin, wind in her hair.

'Come on, girl, let's go.'

BUSHFIRE SURVIVAL!

Every year, brave firefighters throughout Australia work tirelessly to bring bushfires under control over the summer months. These fires can be devastating to rural communities in particular, and the amount of wildlife injured or killed by fire is heartbreaking. In the past, most bushfires were caused by lightning; however, now a great majority of fires are caused deliberately or accidentally.

The most important thing to do in a fire is to keep safe with your family and prepare your properties and pets in the case of a fire warning. Horses become easily frightened in fire, and if you cannot move them to a safer place, they must be contained to avoid them causing injury to firefighters, other members of the public or themselves. A large dirt or sand area with a border of sand or stones is the safest option, away from trees and other vegetation. Remove their halters or replace with leather ones that cannot burn and melt against their skin and ensure there is a sufficient water supply. If you have time, wet as much of their area as you can to stop fire spreading. If your horse is microchipped, it will make identification easier should they escape from their secure area. Have a fire survival plan, and pin it to the wall of your tack shed or another easy to find place, and make sure you have a horse first aid kit in case of injury.

If you find an injured wild animal such as a koala, possum or kangaroo, approach with caution and make sure you have an adult with you at all times. Wild animals might look cute and cuddly, but they have sharp claws and can be even more dangerous if they're frightened and/or in pain. Contact your local wildlife centre or carer to ask for help, and don't put yourself in danger. Remember that wild animals aren't used to humans, so being careful is very important.

Next time you hear about a scary bushfire blaze, take time to think about how amazing the Australian firefighters are. Every single firefighter deserves our thanks for their incredible work, including those brave people who work on a volunteer basis!

ABOUT THE AUTHOR

As a horse-crazy girl, Soraya dreamed of owning her own pony and riding every day. For years, pony books like *The Saddle Club* had to suffice, until the day she finally convinced her parents to buy her a horse. There were plenty of adventures on horseback throughout her childhood, and lots of stories scribbled in notebooks, which eventually became inspiration for Soraya's very own pony series. Soraya now lives with her husband and children on a small farm in her native New Zealand, surrounded by four-legged friends and still vividly recalling what it felt like to be 12 years old and head over heels in love with horses.

HORSE SENSE

Horses can sense the way a person feels, and a rider with a fast heartbeat can make their horse nervous and extra spooky, because it elevates the horse's own heartbeat! There is even evidence to suggest that a horse can start to synchronise their heartbeat to a person they are emotionally bonded to, with the horse reacting both positively and negatively to their owner's moods and attitudes. When you're working with your horse, you will notice that the calmer and more relaxed you are, the calmer your horse will be.

Cody is an English Riding Pony (also known as a British Riding Pony). This breed was originally derived in the United Kingdom from the most suitable Thoroughbred, Arabian and native pony breeds. They are known for being excellent show ponies with stunning paces and willing temperaments for young riders.

PONY DETECTIVES

Poppy is thrilled to be back doing the one
thing she loves – riding horses at Starlight Stables –
especially when her aunt and uncle make all her
dreams come true with a gift of her very own horse.
But there's a catch . . . Poppy must look after the new
scholarship girls. Will the bold and troublesome
Milly and shy, sensible Katie be the pony-mad
friends she's always hoped for? When horses go
missing from the local farms, Poppy worries about
Crystal, her new horse. Will the girls be able to
protect their ponies from the horse thief and find
the missing horses at the same time?

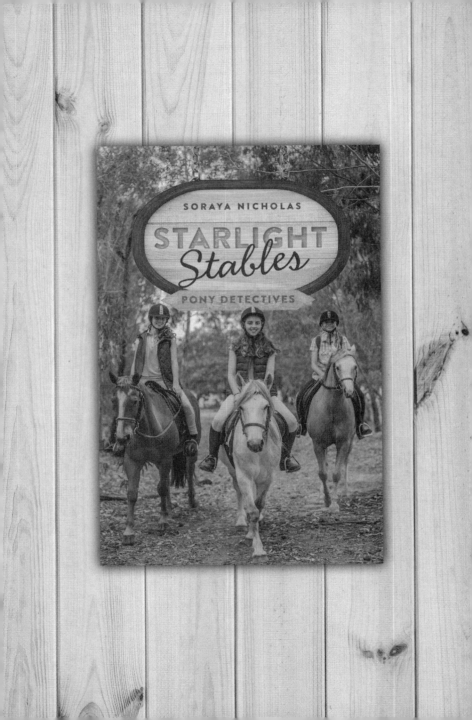

GYMKHANA HIJINKS

Horse-mad friends Poppy, Milly and Katie
are overjoyed to be back at Starlight Stables and
spending every second with their new ponies –
riding, training and having fun while preparing
for their first big Pony Club competition. But when
a rival competitor arrives one day to train with them,
trouble seems to seek the girls out at every turn.
Is it just coincidence? Or is someone trying to
sabotage the three friends' chances of winning?
Can Poppy, Milly and Katie expose their
rival's risky antics in time to save their
chances at the gymkhana?

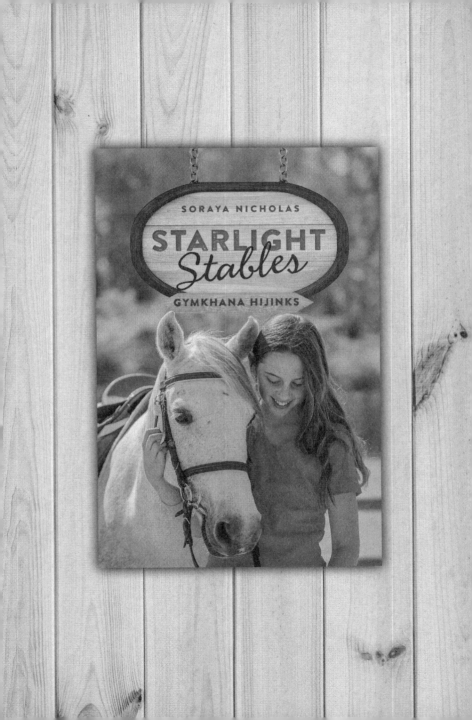

SAVING STARLIGHT

Poppy's world is falling apart. Her aunt and
uncle have had an ominous visit from the bank
and they have lost an important riding sponsor.
It means they might have to sell Starlight Stables.
Could Poppy be about to lose everything –
her beloved Starlight Stables, her beautiful horse
Crystal, her friends Milly and Katie? And will her
aunt have to give up her Olympic dreams?
Poppy is determined to do everything she can
to help. She just *has* to win the upcoming show-
jumping competition so she can give them the prize
money. But it means she will have to jump higher
than she ever has before to save everything she loves.

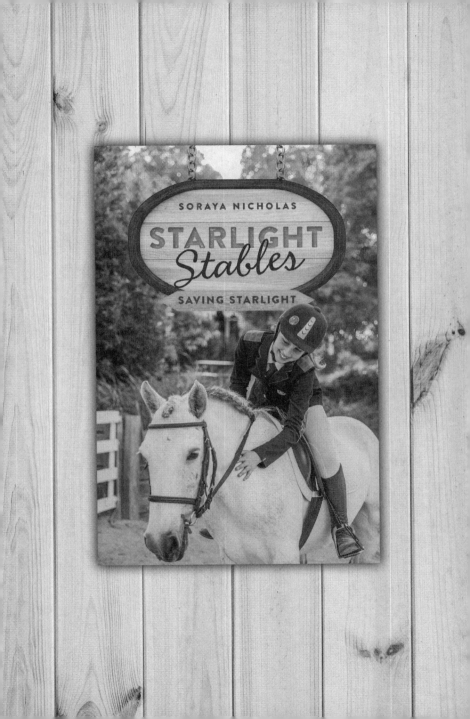

ACKNOWLEDGEMENTS

Penguin Random House would like to give special thanks to Isabella Carter, Emily Mitchell and India James Timms – the faces of Poppy, Milly and Katie on the book covers.

Special thanks must also go to Trish, Caroline, Ben and the team at Valley Park Riding School, Templestowe, Victoria, for their tremendous help in hosting the photoshoot for the covers at Valley Park, and, of course, to the four-legged stars: Alfie and Joe from Valley Park Riding School, and Carinda Park Vegas and his owner Annette Vellios.

Thank you, too, to Caitlin Maloney from Ragamuffin Pet Photography for taking the perfect shots that are the covers.

FOR MORE INFORMATION ABOUT THE

STARLIGHT STABLES
Series

DON'T FORGET TO VISIT

www.sorayanicholas.com